C000091277

SNOWFLAKES AND SPARKS

OLD PINE COVE #1

by

SOPHIE-LEIGH
ROBBINS

Snowflakes and Sparks (Old Pine Cove #1)

© 2019 Sophie-Leigh Robbins

All Rights Reserved.

Cover design by Joey Van Olden

Editing by Serena Clarke

This is a work of fiction. Names, characters, businesses, places, events and incidents are either the products of the author's imagination or used in a fictitious manner. Any resemblance to actual persons, living or dead, or actual events is purely coincidental.

All rights reserved. No part of this publication may be reproduced, distributed, or transmitted in any form or by any means, including photocopying, recording, or other electronic or mechanical methods, without the prior written permission of the publisher, except in the case of brief quotations embodied in critical reviews and certain other non-commercial uses permitted by copyright law.

To my grandmother. Thank you! This one is for you.

CONTENTS

CHAPTER ONE

"Do you think there's such a thing as too much fake snow?" I took a step back to get a proper look at the window display I had just put the finishing touches on.

Even though Christmas was still weeks away, the holiday season was in full swing and Got It Covered was bustling with shoppers every day. It was my job to make sure the entire bookstore looked like a true-to-life winter wonderland. I might have gone a bit overboard with the snow can, though. The big shiny baubles, gingerbread men and candy canes were all covered in a mist of sparkling white. Then again, Los Angeles hardly stood a chance of experiencing a white Christmas, so Got It Covered was the perfect place for people to get a taste of that holiday magic.

"Suzie, there's no such thing as too much fake snow. This looks gorgeous," my colleague Dean said, motioning to the window display.

"You're not just saying that because we're friends, are you? If it looks like crap, you're obliged to tell me."

Dean put a hand on his hip. "I swear it looks good. Now stop doubting your fake snow abilities."

"I guess you're right."

"As always," he said with a smile. "But you did forget to put this snow globe in the window display."

He reached into the box at our feet and tried to hand me a snow globe. Inside the globe was a miniature version of Got It Covered, flanked by two smiling reindeer.

I shook my head and threw him an apologetic smile. "Sorry, I don't handle snow globes."

He frowned, turning the item around in his hands. "Why not?"

"They break way too easily," I said with a shrug, even though that wasn't the real reason why I didn't want to come within a ten-mile radius of a snow globe.

"Okay, I'll do it then. But I do think it's weird that you're afraid of touching the thing." Dean turned around and put the snow globe on the shelf in the window display.

"I don't want to make any mistakes or jeopardize my job by breaking stuff. You know how much I love working here."

He stepped back into the store. "No one's going to fire you for breaking a snow globe, hon. What you need is some perspective. Live a little. Go on a date. You spend all your time in this bookstore. And even though I admire your work ethic, I think you're setting yourself up for a life without love."

"That's not true. I go on dates," I said, capping the can of fake snow.

Dean furrowed his brows. "Oh yeah? When's the last time you went on one?"

"March, I think?"

"Girl, it's December."

"I know. Can you believe it's the end of the year already?" I asked, trying to steer the conversation away from my nonexistent love life. "I feel like summer has only just ended. I haven't even lost the holiday weight from last Christmas."

Of course, I hadn't even tried to lose the few extra pounds that sat snug on my hips. Giving up chocolate chip cookies was a sacrifice I wasn't ready to make.

"Maybe we're getting old. I read somewhere that the older you get, the faster time goes."

I gave Dean a gentle push. "Speak for yourself, grandpa. We're twenty-eight. As in, not old. Besides, it means that I've already had the privilege of celebrating Christmas twenty-eight times. That's not too shabby," I said, even though there was one Christmas in particular I'd rather have erased from my memory. Unfortunately, the medical field wasn't advanced enough yet to make my wishes come true.

"Sure, if you have the possibility of spending the holidays alone, then yes, Christmas is great," Dean said as I handed him a box of leftover decorations. "Which reminds me, I still have to put my employee's discount to good use and stock up on a pile of books."

I locked the window display and stepped back into the store. "You do know that no one is forcing you to use that discount, right?"

Dean sighed. "You clearly haven't met my family. If you'd ever had the horrible privilege of spending the holidays with them, you'd be stocking up on books as well. And tequila. I swear it's the only way to tune out their ridiculous conversations."

I felt a pang of disappointment wash over me as I thought about my own plans for the holidays. My sister was about to give birth and my parents had decided to visit her instead of the other way around, as she couldn't fly anymore at this stage of her pregnancy. They did ask me to come along, but I couldn't possibly skip the busiest weeks of the year when I was this close to being promoted to store manager. We could always have a belated Christmas party once the holiday madness had passed and my sister had adjusted to life with a baby.

The cheerful tune of my work phone distracted me from my musings.

"Suzie speaking."

"Hey Suzie, it's Kate. Could you please drop by my office after you're finished with the window display? I'd like to discuss an interesting opportunity with you."

"Of course, I'll be right there."

I turned to Dean with a big smile on my face. "Kate just

asked me to talk about an opportunity with her."

"She's so going to give you that promotion," he said. His eyes were twinkling with expectation. "How do you feel?"

"Like I've forgotten how to breathe. I can't believe it's finally happening. I knew that Linda was about to retire, but I never thought it would happen this fast. Wasn't she supposed to stay on until February?"

"Oh, honey, what does it matter? The important thing is that you're getting her job."

I took a deep breath. "How does my hair look? Do I have any stains on my shirt?"

Dean placed his hands on my shoulders. "Relax. You look perfectly fine, as always. You can do this."

"You're right. I have to stay calm. I've got this."

"Now go before she thinks you don't care about being promoted," Dean said and ushered me toward the stairs leading to the store's offices.

"I'm buying you drinks at the Velvet Straw tonight to celebrate, okay?" I said, grinning.

Dean gave me a thumbs up. "You're on."

I counted to three before descending the stairs. Kate's door was left ajar and I gave it a gentle knock.

"Come in."

I swung the door open, then closed it behind me, nerves racing through me.

"Take a seat," Kate said, not taking her eyes off her computer screen. "You'd think they'd make these ordering systems easy. I can't get rid of this list of books I selected by accident. No matter where I click, the column won't budge. What if we end up with five hundred of these in all of our stores? Nobody will want to buy a book with a butt-ugly cover like this," she said, wrinkling her nose.

I got up and went over to her side of the desk. "May I?"

"Please. If you know of a way to get them removed from the order list, I'd be thrilled."

After a few clicks, I had deleted the books from the ordering system. "There you go. All fixed. Now you won't ever have to look at those covers again."

I walked back to the other side of the desk, seating myself in one of the comfy plush chairs opposite my boss. "Thank you, Suzie. This is the exact reason why I wanted to discuss this opportunity with you. I need someone who's hands on, knows the systems, is good with customers and isn't afraid to take the initiative."

I nodded. "I can absolutely relate to all of those things."

"I'll be honest with you. Managing a big national book chain isn't always easy, but I love the fact that I have fantastic employees like you to help me build this chain into the best in the country."

"I'm pretty sure we're high up the ladder already," I said. Got It Covered was an innovative and classy bookstore – at least that's what the *L.A. Times* had called it multiple times before. Our stores had a luxurious yet homey feel to them, and our L.A. branch hosted a lot of exclusive book signings with famous authors and celebrities. Apart from books, we also offered e-readers, stationery and a bespoke line of gorgeous accessories like literary-themed mugs and posters. Like our billboards stated, we were every book lover's dream.

"We're doing great, but I like to keep my feet on the ground," Kate said. "Things can change overnight in this industry, so we need to stay on top of things. Having an immaculate reputation is wonderful, but we need to keep the momentum going. Expansion and innovation are two key factors I want to focus on."

I nodded. "Absolutely."

"How would you like to be store manager, Suzie?" she asked me.

I fist-pumped the air before realizing that might be inappropriate. "It would be a dream come true."

Kate sighed and leaned back in her chair. "You can't believe how happy I am to hear you say that. It's bad enough that one of our employees died. I wouldn't know what to do if you'd said no."

A pit formed in my stomach. "Linda is dead? But I just saw her this morning."

I wondered what could've possibly happened to her between nine a.m. and now that had killed her.

"Linda?" Kate frowned. "She's still alive and kicking, don't you worry about her. Linda is a tough cookie. I'm talking about..." She let her gaze wander over a letter on her desk. "Claire. Yes. Claire Wilson from our store in Old Pine Cove. Poor thing died in a skiing accident."

"Old Pine Cove, Wisconsin?"

"That's the one. Apparently the town is known for its ski resorts and snow globe industry."

"Ski resorts and snow globes," I repeated back to her. *And Alex Denverton.*

"Look, I know this comes out of the blue, and it might be far away," Kate said with a look of concern on her face, probably because I was giving her a top-notch impression of a deer in headlights. "But if you could help me out here, the board will be impressed and I promise you that it will help tremendously with landing Linda's job. After she retires, of course. The Old Pine Cove bookstore has only been open for six months. We've pumped a lot of money into it. It's a small town, but a lot of tourists love going there to buy exclusive snow globes. Plus, they all need to have something to read on those cold winter nights or lazy spring mornings."

I nodded, still not able to utter any words.

"Why don't you think it over and let me know your answer by tomorrow morning? And remember, it'll only be a temporary thing until we find a replacement. All I'm asking for is some patience. This time of year is not the best period to find someone who's in need of a job in a small town and who also happens to have the right qualifications. It would be great to have you hold down the fort for us while we start looking for a suitable candidate. I believe you have the potential to turn it into a lucrative store before handing it over to the new store manager. So, see you tomorrow?"

"Okay," I uttered and got up. I made my way to the bathroom where I splashed some water on my face. Not that it made any difference. My heart kept beating just as fast, with or without copious amounts of water landing on my face.

They wanted me to become the temporary store manager in Old Pine Cove? It was the one place on earth I'd sworn I would never return to. Of all the places Kate could've sent me to, Old Pine Cove was it?

This had to be some weird universal fluke. Managing a small-town bookstore sounded like a fun challenge and right up my alley. But the Old Pine Cove part? That made me sick to my stomach.

The rest of the day went by in a blur. It was almost eight at night when Dean and I were finally seated at a table in The Velvet Straw.

"I really don't see the problem, honey," Dean said, dipping some chips into our shared bowl of salsa. "You go to that sleepy town for a few weeks, surround yourself with real snow instead of the fake kind, take some skiing lessons on the weekend or go ice skating. And when you return to sunny L.A., you get that promotion. Plus, it'll be great for boosting your Instagram profile. Just think about all the gorgeous pictures you'll be able to take. What's so difficult about this decision?"

"I don't think you understand. I can't do it. I've been there once before and it's not everything you make it out to be."

Dean laughed. "What are you talking about? It's not like Kate's asked you to go to the fiery pits of Mordor."

"Let me put it this way. I'd rather drink a pitcher of poison while hiking to Mordor than return to Old Pine Cove," I said, taking a large gulp of my cocktail.

"Wow, these Old Pine Cove villagers must've made quite the impression on you back in the day. Were they all serial killers or something? Did they fold back the spines of their books like savages?"

"No. They were a nice bunch of people. I don't know what their book treatment habits are like, though."

"Then what's the big deal? You're not making any sense, honey."

"Well, maybe you should go then," I said, hoping he'd agree and nothing would have to change for me.

Dean laughed so hard, he almost choked on a handful of nacho chips. "Me? You know that the only snow I tolerate is the fake kind."

"It would be a great way to escape Christmas with your family," I said.

"Nice try, but I'm not traveling north during the winter months. Just let me in on the dirt of why you don't want to go back to Old Pine Cove. Please?" he added.

I fidgeted with my paper napkin. I'd never told anyone about my experience there and my friend Rachel had promised me she'd never reveal anything about it either. But Dean wasn't going to let this go.

"Let's just say that something happened there when I was seventeen. Something so embarrassing that I can never show my face in Old Pine Cove again."

I downed my cocktail and placed it back on the little white napkin.

Dean leaned in, his gaze full of anticipation. "You've got to give me more details than that, hon."

"I don't want to talk about it."

He held his hands up. "Fine. Suit yourself. But I can't help you make an informed decision without all the information. That means you can't come crying if you don't get old Linda's job, all because of some silly thing you did when you were a teenager."

I sighed. Maybe I could give him the basics, nothing more.

"Promise not to tell anyone?"

Dean pretended to lock his mouth and dramatically threw away the non-existent key.

"The Christmas before college, I went on a trip to Old Pine Cove with my friend Rachel and her parents. We signed up for skiing lessons and one of the guys there caught my attention. Alex Denverton. He was kind of a nerd, but in a cute way, not in the awkward I-know-every-Linux-joke-in-the-world kind of way."

"This sounds more like a story about how you lost your virginity," Dean said.

"Oh, we're not at the good bits yet. Trust me," I said, cringing at the memory of what had happened next. "Besides, I didn't lose my virginity until I was in college."

"Okay, so you met this dude, something happened, and it didn't involve losing your virginity. So what did happen then? Did he push you down the mountain?"

I bit my lip. "Two days before we had to go back to California, Alex said we could help him with the preparations for the annual Snow Ball. He needed to pick up a pallet of snow globes that would be auctioned off for a good cause.

The proceedings were meant to go to a summer camp for disabled children."

"Meant to?" Dean raised his left eyebrow.

"I wanted to impress Alex and lied to him about having a driver's license. We hit some black ice and crashed right into the town square where the tent for the Snow Ball had just been assembled."

"You didn't."

"And then—"

"Wait, it gets worse?" Dean cut me off. "How can it get worse than that?"

"We got out of the truck, but I had forgotten to put the vehicle in park. It got away from us and crashed straight into the town's coffee shop, breaking our cargo as well as his truck."

"So you didn't only crash some poor guy's truck, you also broke a ton of snow globes that were meant to be sold for a good cause?"

Tears welled up in my eyes. "I know. I can't go back there, especially not at Christmas time."

"Oh, Suze, how long has it been? Ten years? A lot can happen in ten years. People forget, people move to more interesting places, people die. You're not going to let one mistake you made as a teenager stop you from reaching your adult dreams, right?"

"Maybe Kate will give me Linda's job regardless of what I do."

"And what if she doesn't? You know that she doesn't have the last say in this, the board does. Look, you've worked way too hard for this. Plus, getting that promotion would also mean you can finally afford quality food. And then you can stop ordering takeout from that place on Eleventh Street. Their sushi tastes like rubber," Dean said, scrunching his nose.

"You're right, that's my number one motivation for wanting to move up the corporate ladder," I said.

I stared at the melted ice cubes in my drink. Dean was right, but I had promised myself I'd never go back. I was positive the people of Old Pine Cove didn't want to see me again either. Especially not Alex. I hadn't told Dean the whole truth, but me crashing Alex's car was nothing compared to how I had broken his heart afterward.

"Just rip the Band-Aid off and give Kate a call. I swear I don't believe you'll run into any trouble during your short stay in that town. If you do, hit me up and I'll support you."

"I thought you hated snow?"

"I'll support you from afar. Obviously, I won't come and save you while the temperature is below forty degrees," Dean said. "Sorry."

I wondered how on earth I would decide what I'd tell Kate the next day. Should I pack my bags or stay put?

Staying in L.A. could mean not getting the job I had been dreaming of for years. The board wanted someone who was dedicated and had experience managing a store. But going to Old Pine Cove would mean having to face Alex again. If he still lived there of course.

"Well? Should I flip a coin for you?" Dean asked.

I shook my head. "No. I think I know what I'm going to do."

I just hoped I wouldn't regret my decision.

CHAPTER TWO

One short week later, I was parked at the side of the road in snowy Wisconsin. Dean had been right. I couldn't let one mistake I made years ago stand between me and my dreams. So what if this whole endeavor made my stomach twist and turn? I was sure my time here would be over *in a jiffy*, as my dentist liked to tell me before a painful five minutes of deep cleaning. And if Alex was still living in Old Pine Cove, I'd just never leave the bookstore and get a pizza delivered every night. It was the best way to avoid him. Easy peasy.

But before I could indulge in a slice of hot pizza, I had to actually make it to Old Pine Cove before my limbs froze off. After going in circles for way too long, I still couldn't figure out what road to take. I hoped it was a sign from the gods, telling me to give up already and return home to California.

I turned my old-school map ninety degrees and sighed. If only I could've swapped the frustration of a paper map for the gloriousness that was the internet and map apps. But no such luck was on my side. It turned out that traveling back to Old Pine Cove also meant traveling back in time.

The lady at the car rental place at the airport had kindly warned me about occasionally not getting any reception in this area, especially not when it was snowing. She'd urged me to buy a map from her, probably afraid I'd die out there without one.

And now it looked as if I would die anyway, map or no map. I could just imagine the paramedics wheeling me out of there, my body frozen, map still clutched in my hand with a grip so strong and stiff they'd have to break my fingers to remove it. There'd be a young journalist interviewing the sobbing car rental lady, who told the viewers she had tried to save me by selling me a map, but to no avail. I sighed. Was this my punishment for ruining Christmas all those years ago?

While I was battling with the map, I saw a flash of lights approaching me. I squinted my eyes and realized it was a police car. They were going to save me! I fist-pumped the air and leaped out of the car, making *please help me* motions with my arms.

The police officer stopped the car and walked toward me.

"Hello there, miss. I'm Doug. What seems to be the problem?"

"Thanks so much for stopping, officer. I thought I was going to freeze to death here," I replied like a true drama queen.

He threw me an *are you serious* look and arched his eyebrow. "It's forty degrees at the moment. I don't think you have to worry about freezing to death. If that is your concern, then why don't you continue your journey? Did your car stop working? Should I call a tow truck?"

"No, it's just that I'm having trouble reading directions. I'm not from around here. I live in L.A."

Gosh, I sounded ridiculous. As if one's ability to read directions was tied to a location instead of basic intelligence.

"Where you headed?" he asked.

"Old Pine Cove," I replied.

"Don't you worry. The town's not far at all. Fifteen minutes tops in this weather. Why don't you hop back into your car and follow me? I'm headed there anyway and it'll solve your fear of freezing to death." He winked at me, amusement written all over his face.

Even though being escorted by a police car wasn't what I had in mind for my return to Old Pine Cove, it did sound better than spending another hour going in circles.

"Thank you, that's really nice of you."

I slammed the door of my rental car shut. Only fifteen more minutes before I could soak in a hot bath and let all the stress I'd experienced over the previous days wash away. No matter how much I told myself that this work trip was going to be easy peasy, I still wasn't convinced.

I got back on the road and followed the police car. I would've never been able to find the town by myself. Doug turned left, right, right again, went straight ahead, took some more twists and turns, and only then did we pass a sign announcing we'd reached the city limits.

The town looked just as I remembered it. Beautiful snowy mountains made for a breathtaking backdrop. A weathered sign pointed tourists in the direction of the snow globe factory and another led folks to the ski resort and slopes, about fifteen miles to the north.

A couple of minutes later, we approached the town square. I cringed when I spotted the place where I had crashed Alex's truck all of those years ago.

A group of people were gathered in the snow-covered gazebo and as the police car came to a halt, they all turned their heads toward our cars.

One of them got up and approached us. She was wearing a long red coat with a matching wool hat and gloves. She had a clipboard under her arm and a look of determination in her eyes.

"Did you catch a criminal, Doug?" I heard her ask the police officer while she kept staring at me without a trace of shame.

"Just a lost lady," Doug replied with a laugh.

He motioned for me to get out of the car. I quickly averted my gaze and pretended to study something on my phone, even though I couldn't even get one bar of reception, let alone a Wi-Fi signal.

He came closer and knocked on my window. Doug clearly didn't know how to take a hint.

I reluctantly stepped out and greeted the lady in red. She creased her forehead, then pointed a gloved finger at me. "Do I know you from somewhere? You look familiar."

"I believe she's an actress," Doug replied before I could speak. "She's from Hollywood, this one."

"Actually, I don't live in Hollywood," I said.

I explained that Los Angeles was more than just Hollywood and that I lived in Omaha Heights, but neither of them seemed to pay any attention to me. The word Hollywood did seem to have piqued the others' interests. A dozen people spilled out of the gazebo and crossed the patch of snow to get a closer look at me.

"What movies did you do?" someone asked.

"Was it that movie with Mel Gibson?" the lady in red wanted to know.

"No, I'm sure it was the one with that guy from Titanic," another gazebo member stated.

I had to put a stop to this madness. "I'm sorry, but I'm not a Hollywood actress."

Disappointment spread through the group.

"Then why are you here?"

"I'm here to temporarily run Got It Covered."

Blank stares.

"Perhaps one of you lovely people could show me where the store is located?"

"So you're going to be living in Claire Wilson's place,"

the lady in red said.

"It's only temporary," I repeated.

"You do know she died, right? Are you sure you want to live there? I heard the entire place is haunted," she added in a whispered voice.

"Such a tragedy," one of the gazebo members said, shaking his head. "Claire was a wonderful person and now that beautiful house of hers is filled with her lost soul."

Were they being serious, or had I arrived smack dab in the middle of rehearsals for a town play?

"Thanks, but I'll take my chances," I said, hoping that someone would knock me unconscious right then and there so that I didn't have to talk about dead people and haunted houses anymore.

Another wave of blank stares followed. I took it as my cue to walk back to the safety of my car. I still didn't know how to reach the bookstore, but I wanted to get away from the ghost talkers as fast as possible. They were freaking me out.

Luckily, Doug came to my rescue once again and told me where Got It Covered was located.

"Did someone tell you how to obtain the keys?" he asked.

I nodded. "My boss told me that the family next door would give them to me."

"Perfect. Well, have a nice day, Hollywood."

I threw him a smile. "Thanks again, Doug. Although, my real name is Suzie."

"Of course. I'll see you around, Suzie," he said.

I drove away, a handful of people watching me leave. Was this how it was going to be around here? My every move being watched and assessed by a group of superstitious townies?

I pulled up at the bookstore and my heart skipped a beat. The store was located on the ground floor of a cozy-looking house. A big shop window boasted rows of books and a couple of cute notebooks. The display looked dull, but I was sure I could fix that and turn it into something appealing.

A small staircase led to a tiny porch. The front door was located on the left of the building, a welcome mat placed neatly in front. The turreted window on the top floor was flanked by two bigger windows with drawn curtains. Those rooms were most likely where Claire's ghost hung out, away from the prying eyes of her fellow townies.

I opened the trunk of the car and got my suitcases out. Wheeling them up the stairs to the front door sounded easier than it was. Granted, I was only going to be here for three or four weeks, so three suitcases seemed a bit over the top, but I had my reasons. Kate had given me a generous shopping budget for this work trip and recommended I go shopping at Snow Sports Apparel. I'd interpreted that offer as *buy their entire winter collection and then some*. In my defense, my closet had nothing but summer dresses, shorts and sandals. None of those items would benefit me in a snow-covered town.

I left the suitcases on the porch and went to the house next door, where Kate had told me to pick up the keys.

The doorbell made a sound that reminded me of a song from one of those popular sci-fi movies. Star Trek? Star Wars? I racked my brain for the appropriate title, but nothing came to mind. Who was I kidding? I had never been able to keep the two movies apart. All I knew was that they were both located in space somewhere. Fantasy space, of course, not the real galaxy.

The door swung open and a broad-shouldered man stepped forward. He leaned against the doorpost and folded his arms, a smile teasing the corners of his mouth. A mouth I had thought of kissing many times before.

"Well, well, if it isn't Suzie Stonebrooks," he said. "So we're going to be neighbors, huh? By the way, how did you get here? You didn't drive through the snow and crash into something, did you?" he asked, looking over my shoulder to where I had parked my rental car.

I tried to speak, but nothing came out of my mouth. I averted my gaze from his big brown eyes and stared at my new furry boots instead, as if they held the answers to all life's questions.

"What's the matter, Suzie? Can't speak? Oh, I get it. You have a letter for me, don't you?"

Him reminding me of that horrible letter I'd sent him all those years ago almost made me run away again.

I swallowed down a lump of fear and excitement as the reality of things sank in. I was going to be living next door to Alex Denverton, and he looked even more beautiful than I remembered.

CHAPTER THREE

"A lex," I managed to say. "Alex Denverton."

"The one and only."

I gave him a quick once-over. The boy he was at eighteen had morphed into a man. His sweat pants hung loosely around his waist, showing the edge of his underwear. His blue shirt hinted at a well-formed chest and stubble framed his face. Even though it was snowing outside, he stood in the doorway barefoot. He reminded me of a peach. One I wanted to sink my teeth into.

"Are you looking for the keys to the place next door?" he asked, materializing a key ring from his pocket. He dangled it in front of me like a carrot.

"I am. So you were you expecting me? I mean, you knew someone was coming over to get the keys, but did you know it was going to be me?"

He grinned. "Oh, I've been expecting you all right."

I didn't know how to reply to that. What did that even mean?

"There's no need to look so shocked." Alex laughed, raking a hand through his unruly hair. "The owners live far away and I deal with the subletting of the place. I was notified a couple of days ago that you'd take over the shop next door."

"I'm only here temporarily," I blurted out.

"So I've been told. Here." He placed the keys in my hand and gently closed my palm. Even though I was wearing mittens, I could feel his warmth traveling through the fabric.

"Welcome to the neighborhood, Suzie. Even if it's only temporary. I'll see you around," he said before closing the door with a loud thud.

I walked back to my new house. I didn't know what I had thought would happen if I ran into Alex, but living next door to him certainly never crossed my mind. I could only hope he was illiterate so he never had a reason to come into the bookstore. A girl could dream, right?

I stuck the key labeled *Front door* into the keyhole and pushed the door open. The place smelled so musty that I doubted anyone had been inside since Claire died. I threw open some windows and let the icy air travel inside. Much better.

With my suitcases inside and fresh air filling my lungs, I decided to look around the bookstore before unpacking.

I picked up copies of brand new books, their spines and covers in mint condition. I leafed through a book from my favorite author and smelled the pages. There was nothing like the smell of a new book, the anticipation of a new story and the knowledge that you're about to embark on a journey with a cast of unknown characters. One day I'd write my own book. All I needed was time.

The size of the store was nothing compared to the one in L.A., but it had such an intimate feel to it that I instantly fell in love. Small round tables were placed throughout the store, each one containing a selection of genre books. The side wall consisted of bookshelves that ran from the floor all the way up to the ceiling. At the back was a big shelf with rows and rows of notebooks, mugs and pens.

I walked over to the counter and let my fingers trail the length of it. Wrapping paper was stacked neatly under the cash register and little premade gift bows were placed in a beautiful glass container. One thing was clear: Claire had kept the store in an immaculate state.

Fixing the rather uninspiring window display was something I'd tackle tomorrow. First I needed a good night's sleep before catching up on the current state of orders, deliveries and stock counts.

I took one of my suitcases and heaved it up the stairs, then repeated the process. Once all of my suitcases were gathered on the landing, I opened the door to the living area. Or should I say the battlefield of Mordor?

Judging from the state of the bookstore, I had been convinced Claire Wilson was a neat freak. But this room told a completely different story. There was a mishmash of the most repulsive furniture I'd ever come across. The couch had the color and pattern of cat vomit. It made me wonder if the person responsible for ordering the fabric had been high on drugs while doing so.

Stacks of old newspapers, half-opened envelopes and crumpled receipts were scattered all over the coffee table. Its red paint clashed so badly with the cat vomit couch that I felt the urge to shield my eyes.

I made my way to the kitchen, careful not to step into something unidentifiable. Sticky counters and a greasy washbasin stared me in the face, as if they were mocking me for thinking my stay here would be easy and smooth.

I shuddered at the thought of having to live here. This place needed some serious TLC. I scoured the cabinets for garbage bags or detergent, but all I could find were ancient-looking dishes, mismatched cutlery and a half-eaten package of cereal.

I prayed to whoever was listening up there that the stores were still open so that I could give this house a good scrubbing. I also wanted to buy a fresh pair of bed sheets, just to be on the safe side.

I stashed my keys in my coat pocket and made my way downstairs to go to the local supermarket.

My feet crunched the snow beneath me as I passed Alex's house. I felt a burning desire to look at it, to take it all in, to get a glimpse of what he was doing behind those walls. But I decided not to go there. I had to keep myself together if I was going to survive the next few weeks.

Besides, all he and I had shared was a teenage holiday crush. The promise of something more had been tangible in the air, yes, until I'd crashed his beloved truck and broken up with him by letter. I shouldn't get involved with him, no matter how beautiful he looked. What would be the use anyway? I was only here for a short time and I had to focus on running Got It Covered. There was no time for crushes or flings.

Besides, a guy like Alex was bound to be involved with someone. Probably some gorgeous woman with an equally gorgeous body.

The local supermarket had everything I needed, except for the sheets, but the cashier was kind enough to direct me to a shop that sold bed linen. Sure, the stock hadn't been updated since 1950, but the sheets they sold were clean and that was all that mattered.

As the store owner rung up my floral sheets, the lady in red came walking in.

"Good evening, Milly," she said.

"Hi, Diane," Milly answered.

Then Diane gave me the once-over and frowned. "You again."

"Yes, hi," I replied with a close-mouthed smile.

She stepped closer. "I never caught your name, dear."

I cleared my throat. "It's Suzie."

She kept staring at me and I didn't know what the appropriate response was. Should I stare back? Make a run for it? Call the psych ward?

"You. It's you, isn't? Oh my word, it's you." Diane's

shouting voice pierced the air and pinned me right in my place. She walked over to me and pricked one of her wrinkled fingers in my chest. Her red fingernail looked weirdly terrifying.

"I don't know what you mean," I said.

She put her hand on her hip. "Don't play dumb with me, missy. I knew I'd seen you before."

She turned her attention to Milly and dramatically pointed her thumb at me like I wasn't even there. "She's the one who ruined Christmas all those years ago. This girl right here is the reason we had to move the Snow Ball from the tent to the community center. Now she's here to take over the bookstore. What if she does it again? Ruins everything? I think I need to sit down for a moment."

Diane grabbed the edges of the counter and Milly quickly shoved a chair her way, eying me suspiciously.

"You're the girl who crashed young Alex's truck and ruined the snow globes for the charity auction?" Milly asked.

Ouch. Way to rub it in, Milly. Why did everyone around here seem to have such a good memory?

"Yes, but I'm not here to ruin anything. That incident you're talking about, it was ages ago. I was a kid back then. Believe me, I'm not here to cause any trouble whatsoever," I said, holding my hands up.

Milly took me by the arm and guided me to the far end of the store. "Honey, don't worry about it. Diane can get carried away sometimes, but she means well. Just make sure not to ruffle any feathers and you'll be fine."

"Thanks," I said, not daring to ask what feathers

shouldn't be ruffled to stay away from Diane's pointy red fingernails.

"This town thrives during Christmas and the snow globe auction, well… it's been a tradition for more than twenty years. Some people don't like change, you know? This town has a very tightknit community. Outsiders aren't always welcomed with open arms."

I nodded. "I didn't do any of it on purpose."

"Of course. You wanted to impress young Alex. Teenage hormones, am I right? I remember what it was like." Milly squeezed my arm and blushed.

"Right," I said.

I too remembered what it was like to be so consumed by hormones that you couldn't trust your heart any longer. The things I'd done in the name of love were embarrassing to say the least. It didn't help that I always fell for the wrong guy. The married ones. Or the ones who you thought were going to keep a toothbrush at your place, only to find out they already kept one at another girl's apartment.

"Well, thank you for the sheets," I said, and Milly waved me off before returning her attention to Diane, who was still sitting on the chair with a wild look in her eyes.

When I got home, I piled everything into the boxes I'd found in the storage room of Got It Covered. I filled one box with trash and one with stuff that I didn't know what to do with. I would have to ask Alex about it later since he was in charge of renting out this place.

Once the entire kitchen was scrubbed, I made myself a cup of coffee and took a seat in the armchair near the window overlooking the street. Thick flakes of snow fell down and created a fresh layer of white powder on the window sill.

If only I could've covered my past mistakes in a thick layer of snow. The way Diane had reacted seemed way over the top to me, but then again, this town thrived on Christmas festivities and snow globe sales. Maybe coming back here had been a mistake after all.

I sighed. At least I was here to work with books, the one thing I loved doing most in the world. So what if I now lived next door to Alex and thought about what he was doing in there?

I put my cup of coffee down and shook my head. I had to stop these ridiculous thoughts from consuming me. The only reason I was here was to manage a bookstore, not to pick up where I'd left things ten years ago.

I hopped into an ice-cold shower, hoping that would make the fog in my head go away.

CHAPTER FOUR

T wo days later, the store was up and running again, and I had been careful not to "ruffle any feathers". Not that I had the faintest clue of what that meant to the people of this town. But since no one had gotten mad at me since Diane pricked her bony finger in my chest, I was pretty sure I was doing okay.

I'd spent the previous days setting up the window display of the store and scrubbing every inch of the house. After that cleaning stint, the house looked nothing like the disaster it was when I arrived here. I could breathe freely again and was able to shower without cringing. I'd also found a fake Christmas tree and a box of traditional red baubles stowed away in the attic. The tree was now lighting up the store in all of its vintage glory.

Despite all of this, I still felt close to a cardiac arrest. Not because of work. There was an enjoyable rhythm of busy moments and quiet patches. The store was definitely not the problem. It was that damn Alex Denverton who sent my blood pressure to inconceivable heights.

Before I came to Old Pine Cove, I'd had lots of fantasies about what kind of job he'd have. A snowboard instructor maybe. A doctor. A carpenter perhaps. Heck, he could've been a hacker for all I knew. But nothing like this. Alex had turned out to be a prostitute. Or a pimp. Those were wild speculations of course, but I couldn't come up with any other logical explanation for the scene I'd witnessed all day. That was why I'd decided it was the most likely explanation, until proven otherwise.

I'd been behind the counter of Got It Covered for hours, watching women enter his house then leave forty-five minutes later, like clockwork, looking all blissed out and sweaty. He didn't even discriminate. Young, old and everything in between – they all went in and did their thing, whatever *their thing* was.

I was wondering whether or not Alex's nerdy streak was just a decoy for his questionable profession when another one of his clients walked down the steps of his house and made her way to the bookstore with a spring in her step.

Ugh.

I started tapping away on my computer and clicking my mouse like a maniac to pretend I was working instead of spying on my neighbor's clients. When I almost accidentally posted the gibberish my random keystrokes had produced on social media, I closed my browser and turned my attention to the girl who was walking toward the magazine section of the store.

"Welcome to Got It Covered," I said. "If you need any help, let me know."

She picked up a gossip magazine and put it on the counter, throwing me a smile. "I'm okay, thanks. I need some reading material that doesn't require me to think after what I just experienced."

"Oh, okay," I mumbled and scanned the magazine.

"Do you happen to have any granola bars? I'm still a bit weak in the knees from my session with Alex."

"I'm sorry, we don't sell granola bars," I said, ignoring her comment about her weak knees.

"Have you had the pleasure of working with Alex next door yet? He really knows his way around the body," she said while counting her money before handing it over to me.

"No, I can't say that I have." I shook my head and felt the heat spread through my cheeks.

"You should definitely book a session with him. In fact, I've been recommending him to all of my friends."

"You have?" I arched one of my eyebrows.

"I couldn't possibly keep him all to myself," she said, laughing. "Although, you should know that working with him is so intense you won't be able to walk for days. At least in the beginning. You'll get used to it though."

My mouth fell open and a primal-sounding gasp escaped.

The girl giggled. "Don't worry, he's not one of those hardcore guys. He's gentle. Plus, it doesn't hurt that he's such a hottie," she added with a wink.

I had to use every facial muscle I had to stop my mouth from falling further to the ground. What on earth was happening behind those walls? I thought of Alex opening the door on my first day in this town. Him in his sweatpants, his bare feet, and that smile wanting to break free. Had he been in the middle of work then as well?

The girl put the magazine in her bag and pointed out of the window to where a car was pulling up. "Looks like it's Diane's turn. Boy, is she in for a treat. Anyway, I must run. See you next week."

I walked to the window to get a closer look. I didn't care if it was considered inappropriate to spy on your neighbors. I had to get to the bottom of this. Why was Diane doing a session with Alex when she could barely park her car without knocking over a lamppost?

Was Alex getting naked in there with each and every one of these women? I found it hard to believe, but then again, why did they all keep filing in and out of his house, looking so... satisfied?

Diane walked up to Alex's front door with a big smile on her face. I imagined her red fingernails digging into his flesh, and her asking Alex to ruffle her feathers. I almost vomited in my mouth and tried to come up with a different explanation. Maybe he was a masseur? I shook my head. Getting a massage wouldn't leave you all sweaty and unable to walk, now would it?

I fired off an email to Dean, telling him what I had to endure here to get my promotion and explaining my theory. He'd most likely laugh his socks off when reading about my predicament, but maybe he'd have some helpful advice for me, like sealing my ears and eyes shut with hot wax or something so that I'd be oblivious to whatever was going on at Alex's place.

I tried to busy myself by unpacking a box of book orders. My favorite author had written another romance novel and I had devoured it as soon as I got my hands on a copy last summer. Working at a bookstore had the added privilege of reading books months before their release date.

People often mocked my obsession with these kind of novels, but to me it was the perfect way of disappearing into a different reality for a couple of hours. I'd been single for years, and living through fictional characters was the only way for me to experience the thrills of true love and romantic gestures. Not that I would ever admit that to anyone. I didn't want people to know how lonely I felt sometimes. How jealous I was of others who had someone to share dinner with or warm their feet in bed, while I had to make do with TV dinners for one and a hot-water bottle.

I arranged a couple of new arrivals in the window display and put the remainder of them on one of the shelves, but all the while, my thoughts kept circling back to Alex.

All this worrying and speculating and imagining was going to make me crazy. I took a deep breath. Sitting around imagining the worst wasn't going to cut it. If I wanted to know the truth, I would have to be brave and go over there. Not that I'd flat out ask him. I wasn't *that* brave.

I looked around the store and spotted the box of stuff I'd tidied from the apartment. That was it! I'd go over there and ask him what I should do with that box. That sounded not too crazy and totally believable, right?

I quickly made a "Back in five" sign for the door, then put my coat and mittens on. I grabbed the box and went down the stairs, but seeing Diane's car again made me wonder if this was a good idea after all. Maybe I should wait and come back in a couple of hours. What if she verbally attacked me again? I didn't know if that would be the price I was willing to pay to satisfy my curiosity.

As I stood on the pavement pondering my next move, an ear-piercing scream came from Alex's house. Wow. That sure didn't sound like someone who was having a great time. Unless they enjoyed being tortured.

Another scream permeated the air and I ran up the stairs to Alex's house. When nobody answered the door, I put the box down, dug my phone out of my pocket and called 911. This was not about me dropping off a box of discarded stuff anymore. This had clearly turned into a matter of life and death. It was only when the operator answered and asked me what my emergency was that I realized dialing 911 might've been a mistake.

"Uhm, yes, hello, there are screams coming from my neighbor's house and nobody is answering the door," I said. "But maybe it's not as bad as it sounds. You don't have to hurry. I think."

"What location are you calling from, miss?"

"Snow Globe Lane. Number fifteen," I replied.

"We've just had a call from that exact location. There's an ambulance already on its way. I would like to ask you to try to stay calm in the meantime."

"Do you know what happened?" I asked.

"I'm sorry, I can't disclose that information."

I hung up and scanned the road, hoping to see the ambulance approaching. Where were they? I had no idea how far away the nearest hospital was. For all I knew, it could take them an hour to get here.

An unbearable tightness filled my throat. I couldn't stand by and do nothing while waiting for the ambulance. What if they both were on the brink of unconsciousness?

I walked to the back of the house. The door was unlocked and I reluctantly went inside. Turning a corner, I bumped straight into someone. "Don't kill me!" I screamed before I could process what was going on. As my attacker turned around, I realized it was Alex. *Duh*. Who else would it be? The guy lived here, for Pete's sake.

He was dressed in a pair of black shorts, hugging him in all the right places. I wished I could admire his broad shoulders for a beat longer, but my gaze got drawn to the bloody towel in his hands.

"What the freak is going on here?" I demanded to know as if I was some sort of hotshot detective instead of the girl living next door.

"I could ask you the same, seeing as you're the one breaking into my house."

"I wouldn't call it breaking in. Your back door was unlocked, so technically you invited me in. Kind of like a non-spoken agreement."

He grinned at me. "Is that so?"

"None of that matters though," I said, lowering my voice. "I'm here to save you."

"Who's there, Alex?" a vehement voice called from another room. It had to be Diane.

"I'll be right there," he called back, then pulled me into his laundry room. "You're here to save me? From what exactly?" He looked at me as if I'd been sniffing glue.

"Look, I know there's an ambulance on its way here and even though I don't condone your... your... way of business, I'm not cruel. I heard the shouting and thought I'd help out."

"My way of business?"

"Uhm, yes. I mean, you're free to do whatever you want, of course. I'm just not one of those girls." Hearing myself utter those words made me wonder if I hadn't accidentality sniffed some glue after all.

"One of those girls? You don't like to stay fit?" A suppressed smile made his mouth twitch.

"Of course I do. But I prefer other forms of exercise. Not... you know."

He cocked an eyebrow. "Actually, I don't know. What do you think it is I do in here?"

I fiddled with one of my mittens. Was I really going to have to spell it out for him? "Women pay you for... sexual favors." Now that I'd said it out loud, I realized how far-fetched it sounded.

The silence between us came to an abrupt halt when he broke out in hysterical laughter. Tears rolled down his cheeks and he had to put his hand to the wall to keep his balance.

Okay, so I guessed I was totally wrong about him. Somehow, my vivid imagination always got the best of me. It was one of the reasons Dean kept telling me to write a book.

"You… think… I'm a… a…" He tried to get the words out between each laugh. "A gigolo?"

I couldn't help but laugh myself. "I take it you aren't then?"

"Hell, no. I'm a yoga teacher," he said.

"Alex!" Diane's voice was barely audible over Alex's laughter.

"You were right about one thing, though. Diane does need our help. Can you get an icepack from the freezer while I grab a stack of clean towels? I'll be right there."

I scurried into the kitchen, located the ice pack and continued my way toward the living room, where I witnessed a sight that was sure to be imprinted in my brain forever.

Diane was on the floor, dressed head to toe in a hot-pink lycra bodysuit. A yellow sweatband held her hair back and her wrists were adorned with matching sweatbands. Her feet were entangled in Christmas lighting and she had blood on her left elbow and both her hands. To top it off she was surrounded by broken baubles. How on earth had she managed to get into that position?

"You. I keep seeing you everywhere. Don't think I don't have my eyes on you, missy."

Missy?

"This is only the third time we've run into each other, Diane. If you must know, I'm here to help you. Where do you want this ice pack?"

She pointed to her leg. "I don't like this. You've ruined Alex once. Why are you trying to do it again? He's been through enough already."

"Honestly, Diane, as I told you before, I'm not here to ruin anything. Or anyone."

She snorted. "Sure."

"How's it going in here, ladies?" Alex asked, holding a stack of towels.

"Fine," we answered simultaneously. We sounded like two bickering teenagers, although I couldn't fathom what I'd ever done to upset Diane. It wasn't like she was Alex's mother.

"I got you some towels to stop the bleeding. The ambulance should be here any minute now."

"They're here," I said, pointing outside.

Two paramedics hurried toward the house and Alex opened the door for them. They carried a stretcher inside and started to examine Diane, who groaned and sighed with every movement.

"I think you've broken your hip," one of the paramedics told Diane.

Alex led me out of earshot of the others. "I'm going to drive down to the hospital so that I can be there for Diane.

At least until I can reach one of her relatives. We should catch up later though and talk."

I nodded. "Definitely. I'm curious to hear how Diane managed to get herself into a position like that."

Alex smiled and gently touched my arm, sending my stomach into a joyful flurry. "I meant that it would be nice to get to know each other better. Or should I say, again? Ten years is a long time. Plus, I don't want you spreading rumors about me and my so-called pimp activities. How about we grab a bite to eat tomorrow night and I'll make sure you have all the correct information there is to know about me?"

"I would love that," I said.

As the paramedics and Alex headed out the door, an exhilarating buzz coursed through my body. Alex wanted to get to know me better and have dinner with me. And he wasn't a gigolo. This was turning out to be a great day after all.

CHAPTER FIVE

Bells jangled as Alex pushed the door to Dave's Diner open. The smell of onions, fries and bacon wafted toward us and I realized I was majorly overdressed for this place. I didn't know why I hadn't opted for something plain and simple that didn't scream City Girl. Instead I'd chosen an A-line wool dress with black pumps that had little bows on the back. I'd even curled my hair and put it casually up with hairpins. Clearly, my brain must've heard Alex say we would have dinner at the Ritz when he asked me to grab a bite with him at the local diner.

We slid into a booth and took our coats off. Alex was wearing a long-sleeved shirt, the slate grey sleeves rolled up to his elbows and accentuating his biceps. I didn't mean to look at his body all the time, but it was kind of hard to miss.

His eyes rested on me for a couple of seconds before grabbing the menus that were shoved between a wad of clean napkins in a snow-globe-shaped holder.

"What?" I asked. "Is there something on my face?"

"You look nice. Stunning," he said. His smile hit me right in the stomach and made a bunch of little fairies inside of me do cartwheels.

"Thanks," I replied and quickly hid behind the menu so he couldn't see the maroon color that must be flushing my cheeks.

Alex thought I looked nice. Stunning! Okay, so it's not like I could actually date him, but I wasn't immune to his good looks and charming demeanor either. Any woman would be flattered if Alex told her she looked nice.

"Good evening," the waitress said, walking over toward us with a pen and a notepad. She pushed her gold-rimmed glasses up her nose and unapologetically stared at me like I'd just escaped from an intergalactic zoo. "What can I get you two?"

"Hi, Leanne," Alex said. "I'll have the cheeseburger, fries and a Coke."

"And I'll have a veggie cheeseburger." Not that I was a strict vegetarian, but I liked to eat as little meat as possible.

She looked at me as if I'd just ordered a bowl of squirrel soup and then broke out in laughter. "Hey, Dave, this girl wants a veggie burger," she yelled to the man in the kitchen.

Heads turned our way and a wave of giggles and snorts

went through the diner.

"I'm afraid they don't do veggie burgers in this place," Alex said, leafing through the menu to double-check.

"You're damn right we don't. We serve real meat here. Not the fake kind. This has got to be the stupidest thing I've heard all day." Leanne rolled her eyes, not even bothering to do it behind my back.

"Oh. In that case, I'll just have the same as him," I said, shoving the menu back in the napkin holder.

Leanne turned on her heel, muttering something to herself about young people and their insane diets.

"Never mind her," Alex said. "Things here are different than in the big city, I guess."

"The big city?"

We both laughed.

"Yeah, yeah, I know, I sound like a ninety-year-old man who's never set foot out of his home town. I have. At least five times." He winked at me. Those big brown eyes of his lit up like fireworks every time a smile reached his mouth, and I got sucked right into them. The ability to speak or think left me temporarily.

"If I'd known you were a vegetarian, I would've picked another place to eat."

"It's fine. I'm a part-time vegetarian. I guess it's a big city thing."

Alex laughed. "Definitely. You know, if this was my restaurant, I'd put a veggie burger on the menu."

"Aw, that's so sweet. Would you consider adding spaghetti as well? It's my all-time favorite."

He put a finger to his lips, pretending to mull things over. "Yes, I'd give you all the spaghetti you could eat," he finally said.

I threw him a smile. "All-you-can-eat spaghetti, you can't go wrong with that. Now, fill me in on yesterday. What happened to Diane?" I asked, wanting to know all the juicy details.

"We were talking about her regular routine when she insisted I show her a pose I did with another one of my clients. Apparently this girl has been talking about it all over town, so Diane felt she couldn't miss out. I tried telling her a tree pose would be kind of tricky for her, considering her age and the fact that she's only been doing yoga for a month. But she's hard to say no to. I tried to warn her, but she kept insisting. While I was getting things ready for our session in the yoga room, she took it upon herself to try out the pose, without warming up and right next to my Christmas tree! That's when she broke her hip, and got a few cuts and bruises to top it off."

I winced. "That sounds painful. Although I do know what you mean when you say she's persistent. I don't think she's happy that I'm here in Old Pine Cove."

"Why would you think that?"

"The accident with your truck. She says I destroyed Christmas and thinks I'm here to ruin another one."

Alex laughed. "Yeah, Diane's kind of a drama queen. But she's a nice lady once you get to know her. She looked out for me at a time when I was going through a rough period in my life. But please don't give any weight to her accusations. You didn't destroy Christmas. Besides, I was to blame as well. I should've never let you drive my truck."

"Then why did you?"

"You were so excited about it. I thought it was cute, I don't know."

"My parents sure didn't think it was cute."

Alex shook his head. "We all make mistakes when we're young. I know I have."

"I guess that's one way of looking at it."

Alex leant back in his seat. He looked me straight in the eye. "So, what's been going on with you in the past ten years? Crashed any trucks lately? Sent any heartbreaking letters? Swept some guy off his feet who you now share an apartment with?"

I laughed. "Is that your subtle way of asking me if I'm single?"

A mischievous grin crossed his face. "Are you?"

"I am. I guess there was no getting over you," I said cheekily.

"That's understandable."

"I've also never swept some guy off his feet with a romantic gesture. Or the other way around. Pathetic, right? What about you? I bet you're a real heartbreaker."

"I don't know about that. I've had some relationships in the past. Emphasis on the past."

"Someone broke your heart?"

Alex shrugged. "Nothing worth thinking about. Like I said, it's all in the past. It hardly ever crosses my mind."

The look on his face told me that there was more to

it, but I didn't dare push the subject. It was none of my business anyway.

Leanne arrived with the food and gave me the once-over again. "Two meat burgers," she said, making sure to emphasize the word *meat*. "Enjoy."

We both dug in and Alex talked about how he became a yoga teacher. He told me he was saving up the money to go back to school. Apparently he was dreaming of becoming a chef.

I only heard half of it, to be honest. I was getting obsessed with the sound of his voice. It didn't matter what he said. Alex could be reciting the dictionary and I'd still hang on every word. He had a way of making everything sound so… mesmerizing. It was like his voice was a drug my mind craved more and more of.

He took a swig of his Coke. "How about you? Have you always worked at a bookstore?"

"I grew up reading a ton of books. I just couldn't imagine myself doing something that didn't involve books. Working at a bookstore was an obvious choice for me."

"Have you ever thought of writing books?" he asked.

"I'm not going to pretend that writing books and becoming a bestselling author isn't something that I dream of. But I don't know. Maybe someday."

He put down his Coke and studied my face. "Why wait for someday?"

I shrugged. "My job at Got It Covered takes up a lot of time. When I get home after a full day of work, I often don't find the energy to write."

I was such a good liar. It was true that my job took a lot out of me, but the real reason I didn't pursue my dream of becoming an author was my fear of failure. Not publishing anything seemed better than publishing a book people would hate. But I didn't feel comfortable admitting that to Alex.

"I'm getting promoted to store manager in L.A. soon, though. It'll give me more responsibility, but I'll also be able to balance my work days better. I might have time to write then."

Alex raked a hand through his hair, messing it up in the sexiest way. "Store manager, huh? That sounds fancy. How come you ended up in Old Pine Cove if you've got this big promotion waiting for you back home?"

"I guess I couldn't miss you any longer," I joked.

He winked. "Totally understandable."

"Truth be told, I didn't want to come here at first. But my boss was so desperate to keep the store open that I didn't have a choice. I need the experience to show the board that I'm committed. Not that I don't like it here," I added. "It does seem like a nice tight-knit community."

The sound of Alex's phone ringing abruptly cut our conversation off. He answered the call, then after a lot of humming and agreeing, he put his phone away again.

"I'm sorry, Suzie, but I'm afraid I'm needed elsewhere. The Snow Ball peeps organized an emergency meeting at the community center. Now that Diane's out with a broken hip and will probably be in the hospital for a couple of weeks, they need someone to lead the meetings. I can't let them down."

"You're the first person they thought about? Not that you wouldn't do a good job, but why a young guy like you?"

Alex let out a laugh. "I like volunteering. Everyone in this town knows that. So yeah, I have to run."

"No worries," I said. "I understand completely."

"Why don't I walk you home?"

"Sure, that would be lovely," I said, even though I felt the disappointment run through me.

"Or…" Alex said. "You could join me? I'm sure no one would mind."

***

Twenty minutes later, I was surrounded by a team of driven townsfolk who all took their job as Snow Ball organizers very seriously. They were decked out in matching Snow Ball hats and jackets and all carried a clipboard with them. They kept throwing me suspicious looks and I heard them talk – not so subtly – about me.

"What is she doing here? She doesn't even live here."

"Was one disaster not enough for her?"

"It's one thing for her to come back to our town, but showing up at this meeting?"

Like I told Alex before, a tight-knit community. One I clearly was not a part of. Not that it mattered, since I was only here temporarily, but it would've been nice to be acknowledged for who I was – Suzie Stonebrooks, not Suzie the Ultimate Christmas Destroyer. For a moment I considered putting them in their place, then chickened out. I hated confrontations and they looked like an angry bunch.

A guy called Bob opened the meeting and they discussed who would take over Diane's task of organizing a festive Winter Walk through the town. Most of the ideas were turned down because they were either too expensive, too much work or too over the top.

"We need to come up with something. Time's ticking," Bob said, making a tick-tock sound. "A lot of people who are spending the holidays at the inn have already signed up for the tour. We can't let them down. The Winter Walk tradition cannot be forgotten," he added dramatically.

"How about a tour linked to the snow globe factory?" I suggested.

Someone called Tracy rolled her eyes. "We already did that last year. We need to be more original than that."

"Why don't we all sleep on it and present our ideas at the next meeting?" Alex suggested. "As long as we can start working on the Winter Walk by the end of the week, there's more than enough time. Maybe Diane has got some ideas of her own as well. I'll give her a call."

Everyone sighed and muttered, but eventually they all agreed to meet again on Friday with a list of fresh ideas.

I helped Alex put the chairs back in their designated places. We went out and he locked the doors of the community center, then turned to face me.

"Now I'll walk you home," he said with a smile.

Our boots crunched through the fresh snow and I breathed in the crisp evening air. Neither of us said a word, and yet there wasn't a trace of uncomfortable silence between us. It felt as if we had been walking home together for years.

Every single house was decked out with fairy lights and ornate Christmas wreaths. Some people had even placed a nativity scene in their front yards, complete with miniature stables and all. I smiled. The townsfolk might not be fond of me, but they certainly knew how to create a blissful Christmas atmosphere.

"I'm sorry tonight went different than I had planned, Suzie."

We had stopped in front of Got It Covered and the thought of standing close to Alex sent a fresh series of flutters through me.

"You mean how everyone at the meeting made it crystal clear that I'm an intruder?"

"They don't think you're an intruder. They just need a chance to get to know you, that's all. When they do, they'll warm to you pretty fast. Give them a little bit of time."

I smiled. "I hope so. I didn't mind tagging along to the meeting, but I don't think I'll join you again on Friday."

"Just so you know, this is not how I normally act on dates. Running to town meetings and all. Not that this was technically a real date," he quickly added.

My heart rate kicked up a notch. "Oh yeah? How would you have spent your evening then? If this had been, hypothetically, a real date?"

He took my hand in his and gave it a squeeze. His voice sounded as soft as his brown-eyed gaze. "You'll have to find out for yourself someday, won't you?"

Before I could answer, he let go of my hand and spun around, leaving me breathless and alone in the cold night.

CHAPTER SIX

I t had been a couple of days since Alex and I had gone to dinner together and I hadn't heard from him since. I didn't know if he had meant it when he said we would have to go on a proper date. Not that I had time to stress about the meaning of his words. The closer we got to Christmas, the more tourists flocked to the town, all of them wanting to stock up on books and newspapers. If the store could keep this up the whole year round, Kate would be blown away.

It was nice talking to the tourists and hearing about their holiday experiences. Most of them came here every year apparently, because of the Snow Ball and all the other Christmas festivities. An older couple from Florida told me they ordered a personalized Old Pine Cove snow globe every single year, for every one of their children and grand-children.

I loved hearing about traditions like those. My family celebrated Christmas, but our traditions were a bit more plain and simple. Every party started with wine and garlic bread. Then meatloaf with mashed potatoes and glazed carrots. Apple pie and the best cookies in the world as dessert, thanks to my grandmother. And my dad always fell asleep in front of the TV at ten o'clock.

My parents didn't buy personalized snow globes either. Their gifts ranged from socks and scarves to towels and picture frames. They meant well, but their gifts never contained something exciting or surprising. They were practical at best. It would be nice to have a couple of great Christmas stories like some of my friends though. Stories were wonderful for bonding purposes, plus they made for sweet memories.

Maybe… Yes! That was it. The theme of the Winter Walk should be *Christmas stories*. People could go from one stop to another, listen to magical Christmas stories, and enjoy a cup of hot chocolate or mulled wine, and maybe some cake as well. I could ask Alex to whip up a kettle of soup. If they completed all of the stops, they would get a small gift. An Old Pine Cove fridge magnet or a keychain. Or a snow globe. We could ask for a small contribution for the Winter Walk and donate half of it to charity.

I opened my web browser and started looking for an example of a short but beautiful Christmas story that we could use. Of course, the matching cap and jacket people had to approve my idea first, but if I could provide them with a cost estimate and tangible examples, they would be on board for sure.

Right after closing time Kate called me, wanting to know how I was doing.

"I promise to get you out of there soon, but finding a suitable candidate seems more daunting than I'd thought. It seems no one who has the qualifications to be a store manager wants to live in a small, secluded town."

"I'm sure you'll find someone soon. You did find Claire, right? Before she... passed away, I mean."

"To be honest, she was never meant to keep the store open for long. Our regional manager knew her niece and he told her we needed someone who could start right away. Since Claire had been the head of a library before she retired, it was an easy choice."

"Retired? Just how old was this Claire lady exactly?"

"About seventy-two. Give or take."

That certainly explained the horrible wallpaper and tacky furniture in the house.

"And she still went skiing?" I asked.

"I guess she liked to stay in shape. Anyway, I just hope we can hire a capable person soon. We miss you here in L.A."

For some reason I hadn't missed L.A. all that much. At first I hadn't wanted to return to Old Pine Cove, but now that I was here, I had to admit it wasn't as bad as I'd thought it would be. Then again, I'd be going back to California soon. Maybe I would look at things differently if I had to stay here forever.

"Don't worry. I'm sure people are too busy with the upcoming holidays to be looking for a new job right now. Give it a few weeks and they'll be lining up at your door."

"I know, there's no need to worry yet. I've got a much more important issue to discuss with you. Becca Loveheart is doing a book tour and she'll be in Maine just before Christmas. If we could get her to take a detour and agree to do a reading and signing in Old Pine Cove, we'd put the store on the map. It would be a real shame to have to close the store so soon after it opened."

"Close the store? What do you mean?" I tried to sound as casual as possible, but I couldn't stop my voice from shaking.

"It's nothing for you to worry about. We opened the store as a pilot project, to see if we could get traction in small towns as well, instead of just focusing on big cities. The sales figures of our local stores don't add up to our regular ones. Which is normal of course, but the board is aiming for a slightly higher figure."

"I understand. Please don't make any decisions yet, Kate. I will get you those figures."

"If you could, that would definitely up your chances of getting Linda's job," she said. "I have already written a glowing recommendation letter for the board and I'm quite positive you're the best candidate at the moment. But you know how much they love seeing numbers on a spreadsheet."

"I'm on it. You can count on me."

We exchanged our goodbyes and I switched my attention to my computer. The numbers I had in front of me seemed more than fine. Heck, if I had a business that made this much profit, I'd be able to eat sushi and drink champagne every day while taking helicopter rides over the Grand Canyon. Yet the board wasn't happy enough with my numbers?

I shook my head. Some people were hard to please. Granted, they were running a business here and it would be silly to throw money at something that wasn't working, but the store's revenue had doubled since I arrived. Granted, there had been an influx of Christmas tourists, but it was still a great achievement in my book.

I turned my computer off and changed into my running gear. I hadn't gone running once since arriving here and it was starting to show. The cookies I kept eating at night hadn't gotten the memo that they needed to travel further south. Instead, they had taken up residence on my hips. It was time to let them know they'd outstayed their welcome.

After running for about a mile, I had left the town behind me. The forest lay to my left, almost begging me to step into it. Who was I to say no to a good run in nature? I needed to clear my head.

The steady rhythm of my thudding feet was all I focused on for a while, until thoughts of the bookstore pushed their way toward the front again. Having Becca Loveheart signing books at Got It Covered would be a fantastic opportunity. She'd been one of my favorite authors ever since her first book was released, a romance novel that was going to be turned into a proper Hollywood movie next year.

Meeting her had been on my wish list for quite some time. If she came here, I might even be able to convince her to take part in the Winter Walk. It would draw a big crowd and I was certain everyone would love me for making that happen. Maybe then they would forget about me crashing that precious load of snow globes.

It seemed like Alex had forgiven me a long time ago already, even after I had sent him that horrible breakup letter. So why did the people of this town have such problems with me being here? Of course, there was no excuse for lying about having a driver's license and breaking an entire truckload of snow globes, but still. I was tired of having to pay for one teenage mistake over and over again.

And then there was Alex, who filled my mind with confusing thoughts. I seemed to gravitate toward him like a cat toward a bowl of milk. When I thought of his smile and how it lit up his entire face, my chest swelled with a warm feeling.

But Alex was nothing more than an innocent fantasy. He had a life here, and my home was thousands of miles away. Besides, how well did I know him? Sure, he was fun to be around, but I didn't know any of the important stuff. I was fooling myself if I even dared to think of our relationship moving beyond the boundaries of friendship.

I stopped in a big clearing to take a sip of my water. The cold air seeped through my jacket and I shivered. It was best not to stand still for too long in this weather, so I jacked up the volume of my playlist and started running again.

The snow in this part of the forest was packed so thick in some places that the paths seemed to have disappeared. The sun sank deeper with every step I took. A deep orange and pink glow lit up the sky, and I realized I needed to hurry if I wanted to beat the sunset to it.

Just as I was about to turn around and head back, I saw a deer standing a couple of feet away in a big clearing. I paused my music and inched toward it. I had never seen a deer up close and figured this was my chance. Only, how did one approach a deer? The only reference I had was watching Bambi, which counted for nothing.

A creaking sound underneath my feet snapped me out of my Bambi trance. I looked around and saw little patches of water covering the surface.

Oh, man. Had I walked straight onto a frozen lake? If this didn't scream City Girl, I didn't know what would.

Okay, no need to panic. No one would ever find out how dumb I was, because I swore not to tell a soul about my stupid mistake. I turned around and hurried back, but after only a couple of steps the ground collapsed under my feet. Ice-cold daggers of water hit my body and I flailed around, looking for a way out. If I couldn't be freed from this torture soon, my chest would explode and I'd die.

I willed myself to stay calm and think rationally. If I got in, I had to be able to get out as well. At least I was only waist-deep into the water. After what seemed like an eternity, I managed to pull myself out of the treacherous pit I'd fallen into. I stumbled toward a patch of trees and sank down on the ground, trying to breathe. Tears streamed down my face when the gravity of what had happened sank in. I could've died, like legit over and out. I knew I had to move, but I was afraid of falling into a snow-covered pond again.

With shaking hands, I took my phone out of its holder, which, thank the heavens, was waterproof. For a moment I debated calling 911, but I figured that the one person I knew would help me without questions would be here way faster than an ambulance.

I dialed Alex's number, praying that he'd pick up.

After two failed attempts, he answered his phone and I told him about the predicament I was in.

"You have an iPhone, right? What's the password of your Apple ID?" he asked.

"I'm about to die and you want to hack my phone?"

"Just so that I can locate your phone and know where to find you."

"Right." Gosh, the icy cold water had apparently frozen my brain cells as well.

I gave Alex my account details and told him to hurry. I was afraid that I'd lose consciousness or maybe have a limb freeze off. Or worse. What if I froze, then got eaten by a bear?

It was now pitch black and I was all alone, shivering and scared. I had to do something or I'd have a full-on panic attack, so I started to recite the alphabet.

How much time passed, I didn't know, but finally I heard Alex shouting my name in the distance.

"Over here," I called out to him.

Tears of relief fell down my cheeks as he closed the distance between us.

"Suzie? Thank goodness you're okay," he said, kneeling down next to me. "You're freezing. Here, put this around you." He draped a blanket around my shoulders and I clasped it with shaking hands.

"Thank... you... for... saving me," I managed to say.

"You're lucky that you were able to reach me. You could've died out here." His face creased with concern.

"It all happened extremely fast. I just wanted to pet Bambi," I muttered.

"Bambi?"

I nodded and tried to get my teeth to stop from chattering. "I'll explain later."

Alex turned around, his back facing me. "Hop on, girl. We need to get you to the car asap."

I swung my arms and legs around his muscled back and he started jogging in the direction of the main road. I held on for dear life, burying my head in his hair. He occasionally asked me if I was still doing okay, and with every question I felt the energy seep out of me. I just wanted to get home and sleep. I wanted to roll myself in a warm duvet, like a sausage roll, and close my eyes for a very long time.

Alex quickened his pace. When we reached the road, I immediately spotted his car. It was sloppily parked next to the forest entrance. Tears started rolling down my cheeks, this time from the relief of making it out of the forest alive.

"I know this sounds crazy, but you're going to have to take off your clothes," Alex said. "They're completely soaked and the temperature will only keep dropping now that the sun's down. I brought you a dry set of clothes to wear until I get you into a shower."

He could've asked me to spin on my head and I would've obliged. Nothing else mattered to me in that moment except for not feeling the horrible cold clasping onto my bones.

"I fell into a lake or a pond or something. I just wanted to see Bambi," I said as he helped me strip down to my underwear.

"Didn't you see the warning signs along the trail? And don't get me started on this Bambi thing. I think you might be hallucinating."

I put my arms out so Alex could slide a warm fleece sweater over my head.

"Maybe it wasn't the real Bambi. Sure looked like it," I mumbled as I stepped into a soft pair of sweatpants.

Alex put me in the passenger seat and wrapped a fresh blanket around me before racing the car back to Old Pine Cove.

As soon as we were on the road and the town came into view I closed my eyes and everything went black.

CHAPTER SEVEN

Rays of sunlight filtered through the curtains, making the streams of dust in the room glitter. I did my best to peel my eyes fully open. The wallpaper looked unfamiliar and the duvet I was curled in didn't look one bit like the one I'd bought a week earlier. This one was more manly, though incredibly soft.

"Good, you're up." The deep voice coming from the corner startled me. It took me a few seconds to realize it was Alex.

"You scared the living daylights out of me. How long have you been watching me?"

Alex laughed and moved closer to the bed. "You do have a knack of making me sound like a creep. First you think I'm a gigolo, then you portray me as some psycho who gets a kick out of watching beautiful women sleep."

At the sound of him calling me beautiful, my heart did a little jump.

"How are you feeling, Bambi?" he added with a grin.

"Incredibly dumb for running into a pond," I said. "There was a deer there and, well, it's too stupid to talk about."

"Now I get it. Deer. Bambi. Wow, I'm actually relieved."

I frowned. "Relieved?"

"Not that you stepped onto thin ice out there, but you couldn't stop talking about Bambi and I was afraid you'd hit your head or something."

I laughed. "I didn't go crazy, don't worry. Although I did have the weirdest dreams all night long."

What was also weird was the fact that I had just woken up in Alex's bed, and that he had seen me in my underwear last night. I pulled the duvet tighter around my body, all of a sudden feeling self-conscious.

Alex sat himself down on the bed and put his hand on my forehead. "I don't think you've got a fever, which is good news. Are you hungry? I could whip you up something," he offered.

"Yeah, I could eat. Thank you."

"Great. If you want to take a shower, the bathroom is right through there," he said, pointing to a door on the left. "I've put fresh towels in there for you. I've also washed and dried your clothes so you don't have to walk home naked."

"And you're still single? How is that even possible?" I asked jokingly.

"Beats me. I don't get women either," he said, getting up and making his way to the door.

"Oh, stop it." I laughed and threw a pillow at him, missing him only by an inch.

I got out of the toasty bed and swung the door of the bathroom open. The room was as tidy as the rest of his house. Bright blue towels were stacked meticulously on an impressive wooden shelving unit. Just beneath it was a black laundry basket and I couldn't help myself from taking a peek. It was completely empty though. Either Alex was some kind of neat freak or he'd hidden his dirty laundry from me, which was probably a wise decision. Who wanted their neighbor to see their dirty underwear, right?

The sink was so squeaky clean I wouldn't have minded if Alex suggested I eat my breakfast from it. There wasn't a smear of toothpaste on the faucet or a lost strand of hair in sight. Neat freak it was then. I made a mental note not to let Alex enter my bathroom, ever. He'd get a heart attack just from opening the door.

I stepped into the walk-in shower and let the warm water run over my body. I lathered my skin with Alex's minty bodywash. After a couple of minutes, I started to feel less *I almost drowned in icy waters*, and more like a normal human being.

After towel-drying my hair, I looked around for a hairdryer. I opened both drawers, but no luck. Another possibility was that Alex didn't have a hairdryer. Who knew how he got that thick hair of his to look so good?

I rummaged around in the cabinet opposite the shelving unit and my gaze was drawn to a box that could only contain something small, like a ring or a paperclip or a Cheeto. Who was I kidding? Why on earth would someone keep a Cheeto in a jewelry box, unless said person had a Cheetos fetish?

I closed the cabinet. I shouldn't look. It was none of my business what was in that box. Did I even want to find out the answer?

Heck, I did. It was all I could think about. I grabbed the box and opened it, gasping at what I saw.

Inside was a stunning ring with a giant glittering diamond. It looked like an engagement ring, but that couldn't possibly be it, could it? Alex had never talked about being in a relationship that was so serious he kept an engagement ring in his bathroom cabinet. He'd specifically told me that all of his previous relationships were in the past. *Emphasis on past*, to use his exact words.

I took the ring out of the box and twirled it around between my fingers. A small inscription read *Forever thine*. I shoved the ring back in the box and slammed the cabinet shut as if it was on fire.

Had Alex been engaged? Or had he planned on marrying someone, but never gotten around to popping the question? Maybe he was a Ross Geller, you know, the kind of guy who wanted to marry everyone he dated?

If only there'd been a Cheeto inside that box. Granted, that would've been way weirder, but also less awkward for me. Now that I knew about the ring, there was no way to unknow it.

After some internal back and forth talk, I decided never to bring it up. If I did, I'd have to admit I snooped through Alex's drawers and shelves, even though I was only looking for a hairdryer. Honest mistake, right?

I shook my head. There was no use speculating over this ring. If anything, it showed that I didn't know him at all. How would I? We shared a hamburger and fries once, and he rescued me from dying in the forest. Sure, I had almost kissed him ten years ago, but that was hardly enough for us to start spilling our deepest secrets to each other.

Still, I had a lingering feeling of unease that I couldn't seem to shake off.

Without drying my hair, I got dressed and traipsed downstairs, slapping on my best *I didn't just find out you keep an engagement ring in your bathroom* look.

"Just in time," Alex said, looking over his shoulder and flipping a pancake in the air like one of those fancy tv chefs.

I took in the food that was spread out on the table. "If I didn't know any better, I'd think I'd ended up at a five-star hotel instead of right next door," I said.

"What? The guy next door can't be a lifesaver and a chef?"

"Apparently he can. I need to change my perspective on life," I answered jokingly.

I sat down at the table. There was a big bowl of fresh-looking fruit salad placed between our plates, together with oven-baked bread rolls and a pitcher of fruit juice. A percolator stood steaming on the counter, next to a plate of fresh eggs; sunny side up *and* Benedict. Wow. No one had ever made me a breakfast like this before. Even *I* didn't make myself breakfast like this.

"This is… wow," was all I managed to say. "Thank you."

Alex shrugged and threw me a smile. "What can I say? I like to cook. Plus, I was sure you could use a good breakfast after your adventure last night. Which, by the way, was completely risky and dumb. I advise you to never do that again."

"Yes, sir," I said, making a saluting gesture.

Alex turned off the stove and slid the pancakes onto a big plate. After putting all the food on the table, he took a seat.

"Dig in," he said.

I scooped some eggs onto my plate and buttered one of the bread rolls. The food tasted divine. I'd never realized something as simple as an egg could taste so good.

"You should become a chef," I said in between bites.

Alex grinned. "I know, that's why I'm saving up money to pay for my studies as a chef, remember?"

"Right. Only six more months to go before you can start."

"Yup."

"So, how's it going with the Snow Ball preparations?" I asked.

"We've got another meeting tonight," he said, cutting a pancake. "I hope we can finally settle on an idea for the Winter Walk. Diane told me she was planning on doing the same thing as last year, seeing as it was a success, but I think we could use some variety."

I smiled. "I might have the answer to all of your prayers."

"All of them?" he asked, wiggling his brow.

"All of your Winter Walk prayers," I said.

He put down his fork. "Less exciting, but still, I'm intrigued."

I put my fork down as well and explained my entire idea to him. I talked about the power of stories and how they could bring people closer together. I also mentioned that bestselling author Becca Loveheart might be doing a reading in Got It Covered the same day and explained how she could draw a lot of people to the town.

"And we could have mulled wine and hot chocolate at every stop. We could even offer everyone a slice of homemade cake or a bowl of soup," I concluded.

"Will you be reading one of those stories?" he asked with a twinkle in his eyes, making me almost choke on my coffee.

"I don't know if I'll have time for that."

"Too bad. At least tell me you're joining the Snow Ball planning committee?"

I shook my head. "I think I'm going to pass on that one. I don't feel comfortable there, being an outsider and all. Feel free to take credit for my ideas though. Which reminds me, I did have an idea to promote the Winter Walk and reach more people than usual."

"Do tell. We need as many visitors as we can get. The more people participate and donate, the more money we'll have for the charity. These kids can use all the help they can get."

"I was thinking of doing a book- and Christmas-themed photo shoot. We could select the best pictures, turn them into a calendar and donate part of the proceedings to the charity. I also want to spice it up a little. You know, have a cute guy on the cover instead of cute dogs wearing Christmas sweaters."

"What's wrong with dogs wearing Christmas sweaters?" Alex asked.

I pointed my fork at him. "Dogs do not belong in sweaters, no matter the occasion. Besides, dogs can't read and we need to include books if we have any hopes of getting the bookstore to fund the entire idea. We need a man. A man who... appeals to lots of women."

"And where are you going to find this hot man who loves to read? This town isn't exactly the breeding ground for America's Next Male Top Model."

I fiddled with my napkin. "Actually, I was thinking you could do it."

"You want me to be a calendar model?" he said, his mouth twitching into a smile.

"Yeah, but only to raise money for the kids. Like you said before, they need the money. And it's not as if you'll have to be completely naked of course," I added.

He broke out in laughter. "Not completely naked? Just how naked are we talking here?"

"The details are not set in stone yet, but I can assure you that there will be clothes present."

The outfits I would use for the shoot hadn't crossed my mind yet, but I needed to act as if I knew what I was doing.

I'd come up with the idea right after my phone call with Kate. Thoughts of muscled, bare-chested men posing with a book seemed like something that could garner a lot of attention, especially in a town where nothing exciting ever happened. Plus, Becca Loveheart might be doing a signing, which meant the store was going to be packed for sure and there was no doubt in my mind that every attendee would want to snatch a copy of our calendar.

"You know what, let me think about it," Alex said, pouring himself a glass of fruit juice. "Going half-naked for everyone to see isn't something I usually do. Just know that if I agree, it's going to cost you."

"It will?"

"If I do the calendar, you're going on the Ferris wheel with me. No backing out at the last minute. You know, like you did last time."

I swallowed. Ten years ago, Alex had bought us tickets for the Ferris wheel at the ski resort. I was sure he'd kiss me up there, so I agreed to join him, but at the last minute I couldn't go through with it and we never made it into one of the cabins. My fear of heights turned out to be stronger than my desire to share my first kiss with him. The fact that he remembered had to mean something. Unless he had an exceptionally good memory and it didn't mean anything.

"Those are some high stakes, mister. Never mind the pun," I said.

"That just makes it all the more fun, right?" Alex extended his hand. "What do you say, neighbor, do we have a deal?"

I bit my lip, thinking things over. Then I shook his hand. "Let's call it a deal."

CHAPTER EIGHT

With Christmas rapidly approaching and me wanting to continue the bookstore's increase in sales, I decided to take matters into my own hands. The fact that there had been a big revenue boost over the last couple of weeks wasn't enough. It was Christmas after all, and there was no telling if the increased sales would continue after the Christmas rush.

I'd stayed up half the night to come up with a strategy that could help me save the store. I wasn't planning on letting it fail. Not on my watch.

First stop was the Old Pine Cove Inn. I stepped into my rental car, relief washing over me when I saw that I had phone reception and wouldn't get lost again. Not that the inn was that far away, but still. One instance of getting lost was more than enough for me.

I turned on the radio and cranked up the volume. Singing Christmas songs at the top of my lungs felt extra special while driving through a snow-covered landscape. Celebrating Christmas in L.A. was nice, but nothing compared to the real thing.

It was clear that the people of Old Pine Cove were professionals when it came to Christmas decorations. An enormous Christmas tree had been erected in the town square. Two fake candy canes stood in front of the tree, like swords guarding a castle entrance, and big presents with colorful packaging and big bows were strewn all around. The snow covering the pine tree glittered in the early-morning sun. All that was missing was a real-life Santa and some elves.

The road twisted and turned as I left the town center. Three Christmas songs later, I parked the car at the old inn. The place hadn't changed one bit. It looked as charming and inviting as I remembered it, even though the building could definitely use a fresh layer of paint.

To be honest, I had never been inside, but we used to pass it every day when I was here with Rachel and her family ten years ago.

Right next to the front door an inflatable Santa danced in the wind. Strings of red, green and yellow lightbulbs were wound around the porch railings and a big wreath adorned the entrance. A thin layer of snow covered the porch banister, but apart from that, the entire stairs and porch were void of snow.

I pushed the door open, the scent of cinnamon wafting toward me. I took a big breath and smiled. This place smelled just like my grandmother's during the holiday season. Her baking skills were top-notch and every year she baked cookies and pies for the local women's shelter. Even now at ninety-one she wasn't planning on stopping any time soon, which I could only applaud. We all needed a goal that got us out of bed in the morning and got us moving.

"Hello," the girl at the reception desk said with a twinkle in her eye. It was the same girl who I'd met at the bookstore on the day of Diane's accident. The one gushing about Alex's moves.

"You're Suzie, right?" she asked.

I nodded. "The one and only. I don't think I caught your name though?"

"I'm Addison, but you can call me Addy. What can I do for you today, Suzie?"

"I came here to talk to the manager. I've got some ideas that could help the inn as well as the bookstore," I said, suddenly aware of the fact that it was ridiculous to show up without calling ahead or making an appointment.

"That would be me," she said with a big smile. "This inn actually belongs to my father, but he's retired and spends most of his time in sunny Florida. I took over management of the inn last year. Why don't you wait over there while I finish up on these booking requests and I'll join you in ten?"

She led me to a stunning lounge area where a big sofa took up most of the space. The walls were lined with wooden bookcases and a crackling fire warmed the entire room. I sat down and picked up a newspaper from the coffee table.

The title *Old Pine Cove Weekly* was printed in a plain bold font on the cover and the article placement wasn't pleasing to the eye. The whole thing looked like a school project. Still, I was intrigued by the titles.

What burger fits your personality best? Dave's Diner now has a quiz to find out!

Why issuing speeding tickets at the ski slopes is a good idea.

Should the community center serve trendy lattes, yes or no?

And... Wait, what? There it was, on page five. A picture of me, half a page, with the title *Christmas Crasher Returns after a Decade of Silence*. Were they even allowed to print this kind of article without my consent? Whoever wrote this was going to have to explain themselves to me. I read on in disbelief.

Crashing young Alex's truck... losing a precious load of snow globes... turned up again to take over Got It Covered... can't take any more disasters... scared Diane when she suddenly appeared like a ghost...

I scared Diane? Who wrote this piece of sensational nonsense? And who made Diane the queen of this town? This was getting ridiculous. One crashed truck with a load of snow globes wasn't so bad that it was still newsworthy ten years after the fact, now was it?

Unless… Yes, there was no other explanation. *Old Pine Cove Weekly* was a parody newspaper.

Addison put down a tray and handed me a mug of hot chocolate with whipped cream on top.

"There you go," she said.

I put the newspaper down and took the mug from here.

"Here, grab one of our homemade cinnamon cookies as well. You sure look like you could use one," she said with a concerned look on her face.

"Thanks," I said and absentmindedly shoved one in my mouth.

"I see you've been reading *Old Pine Cove Weekly*." She pulled a face. "I wouldn't worry about it too much if I were you. Nothing newsworthy ever happens here, so when you turned up they must've thought it would make for a sensational piece of reading."

"So you've read it? And it's not a parody newspaper?" I asked, shoving the article under her nose. She took the paper out of my hands and gently placed it back on the table without giving it so much as a glance.

"It's not, it's a real newspaper."

"Huh. Okay. I do not get why everyone in this town relies on Diane's opinions though." The words came out harsher than I'd intended and Addy had a scared look on her face.

"I guess it's because she's old and knows everyone. She's also the mayor's mother, so no one likes to rub her the wrong way," she added with a whisper, as if she was sharing something illegal with me.

"That does explain a lot. I'm sorry for sounding angry. I promise you that I'm a friendly person."

"Don't worry about it. Why don't we focus on something other than that article? Your big idea for example?" Addison sipped her drink, leaving a trace of whipped cream on her nose.

"You've got something on your nose," I said, not wanting her to make a fool of herself later on when dealing with guests.

"Oops." She giggled and wiped the cream away with her finger.

"As you know, I'm here to manage the bookstore," I started.

"Something I'm excited about. I prefer to buy books from a brick-and-mortar store, not from an online shop."

"Me too. There's something magical about picking up a real book and leafing through it before buying it, right? Anyway, the bookstore is doing well, but not as good as my boss had hoped. I want to make sure it's going to stay open after I leave."

"You're leaving?"

"Yeah, I'm only here until they find a permanent manager for the store. I'm being promoted to store manager of our L.A. branch."

"Now that's information they should've included in the article," Addy laughed.

"Absolutely. But like I said, me leaving does not have to mean the end of the store, though. It's such a cute place."

"And nothing could make you stay?"

I shook my head. "No way. I'm a real city girl. Don't get me wrong, I like it here. The beautifully decorated houses, the themed events like the Snow Ball… But I miss being able to order a pizza in the middle of the night or go out and grab a vegan lunch bowl. Plus, it's way too quiet here at night for someone who's used to blaring horns and police sirens."

"I can see how life in Old Pine Cove might need some adapting to when you're used to the hustle and bustle of the city. Still, it's nice of you to want to help keep the book-store open."

"Together we can give the store a boost. You see, I've been thinking about setting up a collaboration program between the inn and Got It Covered. You know how there's breakfast in bed? What about books in bed?"

"Books in bed?"

"When people order a book at Got It Covered, they usually have to wait about two weeks before the book arrives. But I could make a list of fifty books that are readily available. No wait time whatsoever. Your guests could order from that list and get their books delivered to their room the next day. All at a special discounted rate of course. Who doesn't love a good bargain, right? And the inn could benefit from it as well. I'm sure certain people would be intrigued by this unique service."

Addy nodded. "That could work, yes. I have been trying to come up with a way to stand out from the crowd. The ski resorts up the hill are able to offer so much more than we can with our limited space and small team."

"And that's not all," I said, a feeling of excitement building inside of me now that Addy seemed to like the idea. "We could also host a book fair at the inn every month, with exclusive promotions, and give everyone who buys a book a free cup of coffee or tea."

"Those are all wonderful ideas."

"So you'll do it?"

"Why don't we give it a try for a couple of months and see how it goes?"

I smiled. "Really? That would be great. I'll have the legal department draw up a contract and send it over to you as soon as possible."

I didn't tell Addy that my boss technically still had to approve the idea, but I was convinced Kate would be willing to give it a try. She'd told me before that they had put a lot of money into opening the store, so it would be wise to give it our all before giving up on it.

"It's great to have someone like you in town. Alex told me what you came up with for the Winter Walk and I love the idea. Don't get me wrong, the previous Winter Walks were fun and all, but your vision sounds more appealing to me."

"Alex told you?" I asked, one eyebrow raised.

Addy let out another giggle. "It was the first thing that came out of his mouth during our latest workout session."

"It was?"

"Yeah. Are you two... a thing or something?"

I laughed nervously. "No, no, not at all. I admit he's easy

on the eyes, but I'm not interested in him that way."

"That's too bad. He deserves a sweet girl like you. Especially after his previous relationship," Addy said, pulling a face.

I wanted to ask her what she meant, but didn't know if I wanted to hear the answer, especially after discovering that jewelry box in Alex's bathroom the other day.

Addy looked over to the reception desk where an older couple were waiting with three large suitcases. "I need to go and help those folks over there. It was nice chatting with you, Suzie. I'm looking forward to getting to know you better."

"Me too. Thank you for the hot chocolate and the cookies," I said with a smile and got up as well.

As I left the inn and drove back to Got It Covered, I wondered what was going on in L.A. right now. Dean and I had texted every day and he'd told me that things weren't the same without me around. Even though I'd reorganized Claire's living room and bedroom to make me feel more at home, it had only worked partially. I didn't have any of the familiar routines I had on the West Coast.

Back home, I got my caramel latte from the same Starbucks every morning and it was always the ginger-haired Caroline who prepared my order, except on Thursdays when she had her day off. If I ordered pizza, it was always from the same pizza place. Me and the delivery guys weren't exactly on a first-name basis with each other, but the uniforms and their standard jokes never changed, even though the faces did. They always wished me a *pizzalicious* day. That cheesy line brought me comfort and I hadn't been able to find that kind of comfort here.

I wondered if that was the reason I loved Alex's company so much. He wasn't a stranger in the strict sense of the word. He'd seen me when I was seventeen, horrible hairdo and everything. Somehow, I felt as if he knew me, or at least the old me. There was a sense of comfort in that realization that didn't compare to anything else.

As I parked the car in front of the bookstore, I spotted Alex sitting on my doorstep.

"Isn't it a bit cold to be hanging out here like that?" I asked, closing the distance between us.

Alex sprang to his feet. "I've only been here for five minutes. Gave me ample time to spot that loose floorboard in your porch though. I'll make sure to get it fixed as soon as possible."

"You waited out here to tell me about a loose floorboard?" I eyed him suspiciously.

"No." He reached into his coat pocket with a grin on his face and pulled out two tickets.

"What's this?" I asked, grabbing the tickets from his hands.

Admit one, Old Pine Cove Ferris Wheel they both read.

"You're doing the calendar?" I asked.

Alex shrugged. "It's for the kids, right? I figured it couldn't hurt. I do have one condition, though."

"Another one?" I laughed. "Should I think about hiring a lawyer?"

"Ha ha, aren't you funny? Seriously though, I'll do the

calendar if you do it too. Having only a man would be a case of discrimination, don't you think? We could pretend to be a couple and do the shoot together."

"Gosh, I don't know. Wouldn't that be a conflict of interest?"

"Everything in this town could be considered a conflict of interest," Alex laughed. "If you say yes, we could go use those tickets right away. I'm free for the rest of the day and I know for a fact that the bookstore is closed today. Says so right here," he said, pointing to the sign with the business hours that was attached to the front door.

The thought of spending the afternoon with Alex and going on the Ferris wheel with him made me feel all warm and fuzzy inside. Maybe this was exactly what I needed to get my mind off missing L.A. and the silly jokes of my pizza delivery guys.

"Okay," I said. "I'll do it. But I'm not getting naked with you."

CHAPTER NINE

The road to the ski resort was long and winding and I was happy it wasn't me who had to navigate these slippery roads. Alex on the other hand was clearly a seasoned snow driver and had no problem whatsoever guiding us safely up the mountain.

"Have you been to Santa's Village yet?" he asked.

"I haven't. I've been way too busy running the store to go sightseeing," I said, even though that was only partially true. The store closed at six, which gave me ample time to go out and explore the surroundings, but I spent most of my nights on the couch with a book and copious amounts of hot chocolate. I didn't see the point of going out alone in the dark anyway. Books were a much safer option.

"Well, we're almost there, so prepare to be amazed."

I looked outside and the resort came into view. It was huge. I estimated it could easily house a thousand people. I imagined staying in one of the rooms on the top floor and looking out at the stars shining high above the mountains at night.

Tall pine trees surrounded the entire property and a big parking lot spread out in front of the main building. It was almost completely full, even though dozens of skiers and snowboarders kept piling out of buses instead of cars. We had to drive around the entire lot three times before finding a spot to park Alex's truck. Then again, it was Christmas season after all and lots of people came to spend the holidays here.

We walked over to the gondola station leading to the slopes and the Ferris wheel. Alex got me a day pass while I secured a place in the queue to get onto the gondolas.

"There you go," Alex said, sliding the lanyard with the day pass over my head.

"Do you go up the mountain a lot?" I asked, pointing to his season pass.

"I come here at least a couple of times a month. Residents of Old Pine Cove get discounted passes and I love snowboarding, so that's a win-win situation right there for me."

"I haven't seen a ski slope for well over ten years." The queue was moving slowly but steadily and even though I was afraid of heights, I couldn't wait to get on the Ferris wheel with Alex.

"I guess we'll have to return soon then. The slopes are

perfect this time of year."

"I don't know if you remember, but the last time I was here, it became clear that I'm not a talented skier," I said, laughing.

"We've all got to learn. But yeah, you sucked at skiing."

"Gee, thanks."

He shrugged. "You brought it up. It was an accurate observation, so I couldn't disagree with you, right? Besides, I thought women love it when a man tells them they're right."

I stuck my tongue out and pretended to pout, when what I was really feeling was grateful. Grateful for having someone around to talk about past memories and share harmless banter with.

After twenty minutes of queuing, it was our turn to get into a gondola. We climbed inside and seated ourselves opposite a couple of chatty teenagers who were busy taking selfies. I grabbed one of the metal bars next to the doors and prayed the gondola people knew what they were doing.

"Getting nervous?" Alex asked, looking at my already white knuckles strangling the metal bar.

"Why would I be nervous?" I answered, pretending to be totally fine with the prospect of being so high up the in the air.

"No reason. Are you really still that afraid of heights? You aren't exactly jumping for joy about getting on the Ferris wheel."

"You mean the Death Trap."

"Wow, that's some intense language right there. Me personally, I'd call it the Heaven Trap. It offers you such a beautiful view of the world, don't you think?"

I nodded. "Sure. I mean, what's not to like? Sitting in a small steel cabin high above the ground with the possibility of plummeting to your death if something goes wrong. It's every sane person's dream."

Alex put his hand on my shoulder. "Look, Suzie. If you want to break our deal, then I understand."

"I'm not chickening out," I said, even though his offer was a tempting one.

I tried to tame the nerves that were frantically rushing around inside of me, but it wasn't an easy feat. I turned away from Alex and peered out of the windows, the gondola giving me a bird's-eye view of the resort and the slopes. The snowy mountain peaks below looked like powdery treats I wanted to sink my teeth into. Miniature skiers swooshed over the trails, all of them looking tiny like ants on a summer day.

"I do have to admit that this is quite the view," I said.

Alex smiled and followed my gaze. "One I'll never get tired of. I love hiking up the mountain in the summer months as well."

Hiking up the mountain? Just thinking about it made me tired already. Alex on the other hand probably got to the top without losing a single drop of sweat.

The gondola came to a halt at the station and the teenage girls sprung to their feet, elbowing each other and stealing glances at Alex. If this were a cartoon, they'd have little hearts coming out of their eyes.

"Enjoy your day," one of them said to Alex with a beet-root face before dashing off with her snowboard. Their nervous giggles made me laugh.

"Looks like you made an impression," I said.

Alex let out a chuckle. "Maybe, I don't care. Come on, it's time to get you on that Ferris wheel."

The snow creaked under our boots as we walked toward Santa's Village. The Ferris wheel stood tall and shiny in the center, surrounded by food and drink stalls. "I'll Be Home for Christmas" blasted through the speakers and people were queueing to get their picture taken with a red-cheeked Santa Claus.

"Look, they've even got a build-your-own-snowman station," I said.

"And there she goes again, trying to change the subject. But sure, we can build a snowman."

"We can?"

Alex grinned. "Sure, Elsa, after we go on the Ferris wheel."

My heart rate picked up speed as we waited for an empty cabin. I tried not to think about those videos where people fell out of the cabin windows or where the cabins caught fire, but it was useless. My thoughts were drawn to disaster after disaster.

I swallowed down a lump in my throat and turned to Alex. "Are you sure it's completely safe?"

"Why? You think this thing is going to slide down the mountain?"

I gasped. "Is that a possibility? Has that ever happened?

Because if it has, you're obliged to tell me. Like, obliged by law."

He put his hand on my arm. "I was just joking. This Ferris wheel's not going anywhere. Heck, it's even survived two snow blizzards without so much as a scratch. And if you fall, I'll definitely try to catch you," he added with a wink.

"Stop it, that's not funny." I gave him a playful shove and felt something shift inside of me. Something I didn't want to think about, out of fear of making it real. I tried to shove the gooey feelings Alex gave me aside and pretended to check an important message on my phone even though I had no phone reception. I wondered why people around here would even fork over money for a phone plan when they were only able to use their phone like, once a month.

Out of the corner of my eye, I saw a woman walking toward us. She went right for her target and enveloped Alex in a hug.

"Alex, dear, how are you?" She pinched his cheeks as if he was twelve.

"Oh, hi, Helen. I'm good, you?"

She glanced at me with a curious look. "And who is this?"

Alex put his hand on the small of my back. I felt his warmth travel through all the layers I was wearing and couldn't stop myself from smiling.

"Helen, this is Suzie. Suzie, this is Helen, a friend of my aunt."

"Nice to meet you," I said and shook her hand.

She clapped her hands together and let out a contented sigh. "It's so good to see you with a girl, Alex. Especially after… you know, Heather." She whispered the name as if she was afraid speaking louder would result in this Heather girl suddenly appearing out of thin air like Beetlejuice.

"Yeah, definitely," he said, his expression changing from relaxed to nervous. "I'd love to chat some more, but it looks like it's our turn on the Ferris wheel. Have a great day, Helen, and give my regards to Herman."

We stepped into the cabin, neither of us daring to speak. What was I supposed to do now? Did I ask him about this Heather? Or did I pretend like nothing had happened? I mulled it over and decided not to say anything. This was supposed to be a relaxed outing, not a moment filled with awkwardness.

"If we look closely, we might be able to see the resort at the bottom of the mountain," Alex said as we reached the highest point of the attraction. The wheel came to a halt, giving us some time to enjoy the view, even though that was the last thing on my mind. I had no desire to see the place where I could potentially heave my last breath.

I shook my head. Why couldn't I stop thinking about dying in a horrible accident? I was sitting next to a gorgeous guy, for crying out loud.

"So, who's this person we do not speak of?" The question leaped out of my mouth before I could stop myself.

Alex creased his brow. "Voldemort?"

"No, not Voldemort. I'm talking about this Heather girl. Helen seemed almost afraid to utter her name."

"Yeah, sorry about that coming up," Alex said with a pained expression on his face. "We don't have to talk about her, you know."

"It's your call," I answered.

I didn't know why his secretiveness made the little green monster's head pop up. It was ridiculous. Alex was a grown man and he was bound to have a couple of past lovers. It was none of my business. Not that it even mattered, did it? It wasn't like he owed me anything, or like I expected anything from him. I wasn't having *real* feelings for him. A silly crush, maybe. A fantasy never to be acted upon, sure. But nothing more. Nothing to make me feel this jealous, anyway.

He turned and locked eyes with me. "I don't want it to be a secret either."

I nodded and he continued speaking. "Her name was Heather, but you already know that of course. Anyway, we were together for five years when I proposed to her. You see, I was madly in love with her and wanted to fully commit to spending our lives together. But she said no, packed her bags and left. Just like that. It's been a year and I haven't seen her since, nor do I know where she even lives now. Heck, I don't even have a clue as to why she turned me down. I thought we were happy together, but I guess I have poor judgement."

I took his hand in mine and gave it a squeeze. "I'm sorry. That must've been rough for you."

"It's in the past," he said. "No need to think about it anymore."

I hesitated for a moment, but decided to speak after all. "When I was using your bathroom the other day, I was looking for a hairdryer and I… uhm…"

He sighed. "You found the ring."

"I'm sorry, I should've told you sooner."

He smiled at me. "That's okay. I shouldn't have left it there in the first place."

"Why did you keep the ring if you say it's all in the past?"

A sad look crossed his face. "Because sometimes we hold on to something we should've let go of a long time ago."

His words hit home for me big time, with the difference that I had let go of things I didn't want to let go of. Like my dream of publishing a book. I kept telling myself that I'd do it someday, although I knew deep down that someday would never arrive if I didn't get up and do something. It didn't feel good knowing I kept sabotaging myself like that.

And the fact that I hadn't experienced a love like Alex had – where you are so in love that you want to spend the rest of your life with the other person and are comfortable enough to share a pizza in bed after getting home at one in the morning – didn't feel good either. Sure, I had a great job and amazing friends, but something was missing from my life. Passion and excitement to name two. I fought back a tear wanting to break free, and told myself to keep it together. I was not going to cry while I was on the Ferris wheel with a cute guy.

"Look at us being all bummed out," I said, meeting Alex's eyes. It was as if the entire world had stopped spinning for a moment and it was just us two. The cabin hung so high in the sky that all I could hear was the wind and the sound of my own heartbeat.

I realized we were still holding hands, but didn't want to let go.

"Yeah," Alex said. "Although I have to admit that I've been feeling a lot less heartbroken these past few days."

He stroked my cheek with one hand. I felt my insides tremble from his warm touch. Was he going to kiss me?

I felt a craving in my soul, a longing to feel his lips on mine. But that was my heart talking. I had to be sensible. Giving in to these feelings deep down inside of me would rock my world so hard that my boat would tip over and crash.

I wasn't ready to have my heart broken like that, and a kiss would inevitably lead to that happening. Because Alex was here, and I had a plane ticket that would take me back to LAX soon. Plus, he kept a ring in his house that he'd bought for another girl. It was not the kind of situation I wanted to get caught up in, thank you very much.

But the depth of his dark eyes touched my soul on a level I didn't know existed. I bit my lower lip, my hands trembling as he inched closer.

A small, shocking motion took us both out of our trance and I had to grab one of the bars attached to the roof of the cabin in order to stay seated. The Ferris wheel started moving again and the moment passed, even though the air between us was still so loaded that we could single-handedly light up the sky if we wanted to.

"Do you want to take a picture together? Otherwise no one back home will believe I faced my fear of heights," I said, trying to fill the silence between us.

Alex took his phone out of his coat pocket and turned the camera to selfie mode. He put his arm around my shoulder and our cheeks almost touched as we huddled together.

"I'll send you a copy," he said, checking out the result. "If you want to have one, of course."

"Are you kidding me? I'd love to have a memory of this fine day."

We descended in silence, each of us consumed by our thoughts.

"Let's build that snowman now, shall we?" Alex asked as soon as we touched solid ground again.

"Let's. But first I could use a warm cup of cocoa," I answered and followed him through Santa's Village like we hadn't held hands and almost kissed up there.

CHAPTER TEN

"**P**lease tell me you've kissed him. Those lips look heavenly."

"I already told you that nothing happened between us, and that nothing's going to happen, no matter how kissable his lips are."

I was on the phone with Dean, who'd called me mere seconds after I sent him the selfie of me and Alex on the Ferris wheel. It had been two days since we took that picture and the memory still made me smile.

"Oh, honey, you are so smitten."

"I am not."

"Sure. You can't shut up about his kissable lips, but he's just a friend, right?" Dean teased.

I let out a sigh and twirled a strand of hair around my

finger. "Even if I wanted to, hypothetically, kiss him, I couldn't. We live thousands of miles apart, Dean. There's no way this could ever work, so there's no use kissing the guy. I need to be sensible about this."

"Whatever you need to hear to keep yourself fooled, Suze. Anyway, I've got some news and I'm afraid it's not entirely good."

I sat up a little straighter. "What do you mean? It's about the store manager's job, isn't it? Did Linda decide not to retire after all? You know, she's been going on and on about how she doesn't know what she'll do with all of her free time once she's retired. She's going to stay at Got It Covered until she's a hundred years old, isn't she?"

"Jeez, relax, woman," Dean laughed. "It's nothing like that."

"Then what is it like?"

"Kate's been doing job interviews. She told me not to tell you, but who is she kidding? Of course I have to tell you."

"Job interviews? What are you talking about?"

"It's nothing you have to worry about, honey. Kate says it's just a formality. The board of directors was afraid that not making the job public would result in a lawsuit. Equal rights for all and all that."

I scoffed. "That's nonsense."

"They don't want to take their chances. Apparently, some dude sued a grocery store last month for promoting one of their employees without doing job interviews first. The guy claimed it robbed him of the chance to get his dream job and that it was discrimination to not interview people who worked at the store already. He said it was a case of favoritism."

"So you're telling me that because some crazy fool spread around some insane ideas, I have to deal with… competition from outside? What if there's someone more qualified than me? And why didn't Kate tell me personally? It must be because she's got something to hide, right? Oh gosh, this is bad."

"It's going to be fine, trust me. But I just thought you had a right to know."

"Why?"

Dean hesitated before he spoke. "So that you're prepared in case Kate isn't telling the truth after all."

A wave of panic washed over me. "Don't say that. This job is what I've been working for all these years. It's why I'm here in this cold remote town where they don't even serve veggie burgers," I cried out.

"You're right, that is harsh."

I rubbed my fingers over my forehead. "I have to make sure that the Old Pine Cove store does extremely well. That way, Kate won't have an inch of doubt about who to hire for the job. I don't care if she says these job interviews are nothing more than a formality, it's still business. The board cares about stuff like turnover and ROI and profits more than they do about me."

"If anyone can make a success out of a local store, it's you, honey. You go kick some snowy butts out there. I'll send you updates."

"Promise?"

"Promise. Oh, and Suze?"

"Yes?"

"Give that Alex guy a big kiss for me."

I hung up and put my phone on the counter. This was not how things were supposed to go. I should've never left L.A. Don't they say that proximity is key? Yet here I was, far, far away, not able to do anything or talk to Kate in person.

I thought through all the ideas I'd come up with so far to give the store a boost. They weren't enough. I had to think bigger. Bolder.

The calendars we were making for the Snow Ball would undoubtedly appeal to a lot of people, not just the ones visiting the town. I could sell them on our website. Heck, I'd sell them on every continent if I had to.

I opened my laptop and started doing my research. After several emails and phone calls, I had a pretty good picture of the costs involved in printing and shipping the calendars worldwide. Even if we donated a small amount for every calendar sold, they'd still be quite profitable. The photo shoot was already planned anyway, so having more copies would only lower the initial costs.

I poured everything into a spreadsheet and drafted a proposal to send to Kate. I also included a final presentation for the collaboration between the inn and Got It Covered.

I couldn't lose this promotion. It would be as if nothing had mattered. The late nights, the birthday parties I'd missed, the trips I didn't take, the weekends I'd had to work.

No one was taking this chance away from me. I hadn't come this far to be stopped in my tracks by someone who didn't have the faintest clue of what Got It Covered was like. The job was mine and mine only.

***

Later that day, I was about to close the store when Addy and a man I didn't recognize walked in together.

"This is Hugo, a journalist for Old Pine Cove Weekly," Addy said. "He's agreed to write an article about your involvement in the Snow Ball."

"Uhm, okay. But why me?" I asked. "Don't get me wrong, it's a nice idea, but wouldn't it make more sense to talk to some of the locals?" I wasn't looking forward to having my name printed in the local paper again.

"Nonsense," Addy said. "People want to hear about the new girl in town who's contributing without expecting anything in return. I told Hugo about your wonderful ideas for the Winter Walk and how you're planning on selling those special calendars." She leaned closer and whispered into my ear. "It'll make everyone forget about that article they published about you earlier."

"You think?" I asked.

"You bet."

"Well, okay. Thank you," I said and turned to Hugo. "I'd love to talk to you, but first I need to wrap up some things around here. How about we meet in an hour?"

He nodded. "Very well. Would you be okay with meeting me at Dave's Diner?"

I thought back to the whole veggie burger debacle, but decided I couldn't let this friendly man down. He was going to write something nice about me after all and I didn't want to influence his opinion about me. I could always order a double cheeseburger during the interview and impress Leanne that way.

"Sure, that sounds perfect."

"I'll make sure we get the best table," Hugo said, then turned and walked out the door.

"Are you sure this is a good idea?" I asked Addy. "I'd rather keep a low profile while I'm here. I even asked Alex not to mention they were my ideas at the Snow Ball meetings, but rather to pretend he was the one who came up with them."

Addy laughed. "Pretend he came up with getting his picture taken and have his face plastered all over a sexy calendar? That seems highly unlikely."

"I never said it was going to be a sexy one," I said, a blush deepening the color of my cheeks.

She wiggled her eyebrows. "If it was, I'd buy a bunch and give every one of my friends a copy for Christmas."

"We'll see how they turn out, but don't hold your breath."

Addy walked through the store, picking up books and leafing through a magazine. It was clear she was trying to act casual, but I could sense something was up.

"So, Helen told me she saw you and Alex at Santa's Village and that you two looked quite cozy."

Ha, there it was.

"Is it even possible to have secrets in this town? Or does everything go straight to the grapevine?"

Addy smiled. "The latter. There are no secrets in this town, I'm afraid. Unless you do something where no one can see you. Like… someone's bedroom."

"Why does everyone think I've got the hots for Alex? I mean, yes, I have seen his bedroom. Slept in his bed even," I said without thinking.

Addy slammed the book she was holding back on the table. "What? You have to tell me everything. Please. This is the most exciting thing that's happened in this town since old Richard almost choked on a donut three months ago."

"I was just kidding. I mean, I've slept in his bed, but only because he was taking care of me."

I told Addy about how I got lost in the woods and almost froze to death, purposefully leaving out the part where I'd walked into the pond like a dumbass. That was something I didn't want the entire town to know. Then it dawned on me she could just as easily talk about me being in Alex's bed and next thing you know, the story would get blown out of proportion, turning me into a tramp.

"You have to promise me you won't tell a soul about this. Not a word."

Addy nodded. "Of course."

I hoped I could trust her to keep her word. Addy was sweet as a Christmas cookie, but also very talkative.

"Don't worry, your secret is safe with me. I don't understand how you two are not together, though. From what I can tell, Alex is really fond of you."

"I'm fond of him as well, but honestly, we're just friends," I said, even though deep down I had to admit that there was something of a spark when I thought about him. The feelings I had a decade ago came rushing back in spurts when he was around.

"I dare to disagree. Why else would a guy go to all that trouble? Taking care of you, going for a ride on the Ferris wheel, being a model for your calendar… If you ask me, that's not being friendly, that's being in love."

I couldn't help but smile at the thought of it being true. "Who knows? Maybe he's into me, maybe he's not. Whatever the truth may be, thanks for arranging that interview for me. It'll be good to get Diane out of my hair. For some reason, she doesn't like me."

Addy fiddled with a stack of bookmarks. "She's only looking out for Alex. I wouldn't take it personal. Last year he had his heart broken by a girl we all thought would stick around. I think Diane's afraid he'll get hurt again."

"Alex told me that as well, but there's one thing I can't understand. Why her? Please tell me she's not his real mother or something?"

"She's not. They are related though. Diane's a cousin of Alex's mother. Ever since his mom moved out of town when he was thirteen, Diane kind of felt it was her duty to look out for him."

I shut my laptop off and closed it, struggling to keep all of the questions I had about his mother and why she'd left inside of me. For some reason it didn't feel right to discuss Alex's personal life with Addy.

"Well, I should get changed and head over to Dave's Diner," I said, glancing at the time on my phone.

"Let me know how it goes, okay? Maybe we can get some coffee together tomorrow morning?" Addy asked, gathering her things.

"I would love to, but I've got the photo shoot tomorrow."

"In that case, I'll swing by. Seeing Alex half naked is something I don't want to miss. You're one lucky girl."

I laughed. "Enough with the naked talk. It's going to be pretty decent."

"If you say so," she said with a wink before she headed out.

Her remark made me think though. Should I ask Alex to spice up the photos? I had to admit that I wouldn't be opposed to it. I already knew he had a perfectly maintained body, but seeing it up close would be a whole new ballgame. I grinned foolishly as I imagined Alex taking off his shirt and smiling at me. Even the thought alone was enough to make a girl weak in the knees. *Keep it together, Suzie*, I told myself. *For the love of all that's good in this world, keep it together.*

CHAPTER ELEVEN

One hour. That was all it took to transform Got It Covered into a professional set. Pam, the photographer, had arrived with three sets of lamps, two tripods, garment bags full of outfits and boxes filled with Christmas props. I'd watched her as she carefully laid out the props on one of the tables. There were Santa hats, red-and-white striped socks, mugs, antler ears, fake presents, snow globes, a bag full of candy canes and four bags of marshmallows. Either she was completely nuts about Christmas and she'd had all this stuff stacked away at home somewhere, or she'd raided an entire store worth of decorations, leaving other families crying over finding nothing left to buy.

Kate had told me they'd decided to make it a nationwide

calendar after reading my proposal and seeing pictures of Alex. She said she wanted the result to be sexy, but friendly. The photos would all be centered around books of course, but she thought having me and Alex star as a couple would be the most marketable option. Plus, with Becca Loveheart confirming the signing, the store would attract lots of new customers who'd more than likely want to snatch a copy of the calendar as well. Kate had even agreed to closing the store for one day so that we wouldn't have to wait to do the photo shoot.

I couldn't keep myself from checking the time every minute, even though Alex wasn't expected to arrive for another fifteen minutes. I took out my phone and opened the camera app to check my look. I'd loosely curled my hair and had opted for bronze eyeshadow, black mascara and a light pink lipstick.

"This is the outfit I selected for the first photos," Pam said, handing me a garment bag and a pair of black pumps.

"I'll go try them on upstairs," I said and made my way to the living room.

I unzipped the bag and retrieved the outfit. It was a sparkling black dress with a deep-plunging neckline and an open back. On top of the dress rested a pair of stylish red stockings and red earrings. They complemented the look and gave it a genuine Christmassy feel.

I put everything on, then slipped my feet into the pumps. The black leather was shiny and new, a big contrast with my own shoes. The color of my trusty pumps had started to wear around the tips, but I found it nearly impossible to find a pair that fit me like a shoe should fit – comfortably, without giving you blisters. This pair felt different, though, and to top it off, they made me feel like a movie star.

When I arrived downstairs again, I saw Alex chatting with Pam and I walked toward them.

"Hey you," he said, his eyes lighting up at the sight of me. Or it could've been the sparkles of the dress that blinded him. There was no way to tell.

"Do you like it?"

He let out a puff of air and laughed. "Like it? I love it. You look very pretty."

"Thanks."

I couldn't help but smile. Alex thought I looked pretty! I almost did a happy twirl, but constrained myself. There was no need to show my crazy side to him. Not yet anyway.

"I should get dressed as well. Mind if I use your bed-room?" he asked.

I quickly made a mental assessment of the state of my bedroom. There were no dirty underwear or wet towels lying around. At least, that's what I hoped.

"Sure. It's only fair that you get to see my bedroom after I've seen yours," I said with a wink.

I took my phone and fired off a quick text to Dean, telling him Alex was about to enter my bedroom. I loved teasing him like that.

His reply came mere seconds later. *"If that's true, then why are you wasting your time texting me???"*

I selected the selfie I'd taken earlier and send it to him. *"Because I've already put on my outfit. We're doing the photo shoot today."*

"Ask someone to take pictures. I can't wait until the calendar gets printed."

I put my phone behind the counter and smiled. When I arrived here, I was afraid of running into Alex because I was ashamed of what had happened between us ten years ago, and now I was about to take pictures with him and act as if we were more than friends. Me. With a guy who would unquestionably enter the fantasies of women all over the country. I was one lucky girl.

"What do you think?"

I turned around to see Alex standing there with a modest smile on his face. He was wearing black jeans and a black button-up shirt. His red tie was loosened and hung teasing over the buttons, all of them undone.

He ran a hand through his unruly hair. "Is this the look you were going for?"

My heart pounded so fast, I was afraid it might explode. "I think you nailed it, yes."

"Since we both look the part, I think we should ask them if we can keep the outfits for Christmas. The Snow Ball's got a best outfit for couples competition. Might be fun to win it this year. Anyway, let's get this show on the road."

Alex walked away, leaving me breathless. He wanted to spend Christmas together? The thought of seeing him on Christmas Eve had crossed my mind, since we were both organizing the Snow Ball. But I figured it would be more of an informal meet-up, not one where we would wear matching outfits and try to win the prize for best-dressed couple.

I tried to shake off all of my thoughts about what this meant and joined Alex and Pam. She had placed one of the store's stunning armchairs in front of the window, right next to my Christmas tree. A fresh layer of snow painted the background street white. It looked like a fairytale come alive.

"Alex, if you can sit down in the chair? And Suzie, put yourself on his lap."

We did as we were told. I tried my best not to touch Alex more than necessary, but that seemed to be rather impossible as we were in such a confined space together.

Pam handed Alex a book. "Pretend to read this story together. Oh, and we need more sizzle than this," she said, waving a hand at us. "Remember, you're supposed to look like you're attracted to each other. Right now, you look like you both have some sort of contagious disease and are afraid to touch each other. We don't want to send out that vibe, right?"

I inched closer to Alex so that we could both look at the pages of the book. I swung my feet over the side of the armchair and hoped he didn't mind holding me.

Even though the photo shoot was something I'd come up with myself, I had never imagined it would be this intimate.

Pam positioned herself with her camera. "Now, if you could put your hand on Suzie's leg? A lot higher if you can," she added when Alex put his hand on my calf. "And smile, smile, smile, folks."

The more the camera clicked, the more relaxed I felt. This wasn't too bad after all. I just had to smile and stare at the words in the book. I started reading, to try to distract myself from Alex's touch. His hand was dangerously close to the seam of my dress and it seemed to burn a hole through my red stockings.

"Great work," Pam said, lowering her camera. "Let's try another setting." She shoved the armchair to the side and threw a white plushy blanket down. She instructed Alex to lean against the armchair and hold me in his arms, then placed stacks of books and fake presents around us before taking a step back. "Perfect. Let's do this."

I turned my head to face Alex and stared into his brown eyes.

"This is weird, isn't it?" he whispered.

"The things we do for charity, am I right?"

"I don't mind, though," he said and squeezed me tighter, with a smile that made his eyes sparkle. His thumb gently caressed my arm and I could hardly keep it together anymore. A deep desire sprang to life and traveled all over my body.

I let out a barely audible sigh. As soon as this shoot was over, I would have to head outside and throw myself in the snow to cool down.

"You know, after you left that winter, I thought I'd never see you again," Alex whispered. "Isn't it strange to think that you ended up here in a way none of us could've ever conjured up in our minds?"

"Totally," I agreed.

Apart from the camera shutter, there wasn't a sound to be heard. It was almost as if we were the only people on the planet. If I closed my eyes, I was sure that I would be able to pretend all of this was real. Then again, did I want this to be real? Or was it nothing but a fun fantasy to make my limited time here more interesting?

I'd gotten so swept up in my thoughts that I hardly heard Pam say we could take a break. "And you've also got a visitor," she added.

I looked up to see Addy lingering near the door. She was holding a tray with coffee cups, steam circling upward through the slits in the lids.

"I thought you guys could use some caffeine."

"Thanks," I said, getting up and grabbing one of the cups.

"I'm going to head to the bathroom first," Alex said. "Great to see you, Addy."

As soon as he was out of earshot, Addy turned to me. "That looked cozy. In fact, more than cozy. I need every single copy of that calendar, plus details. Gosh, I need all of the details."

"It was... an experience for sure," I said.

"Are you sure there's nothing more there? That this is all just pretending?"

I batted a hand at her. "Oh, definitely. We're nothing more than friends."

As I spoke the words, I knew I was lying. In this moment, we were indeed nothing more than friends, but I couldn't deny that feeling inside of me any longer. It tugged on my insides and set my skin on fire every time I was near Alex.

"He is extremely hot though," I told Addy.

She clapped her hands together. "You two would be perfect together. You should definitely kiss him."

"Kiss who?" Alex had slipped back in. He took a cup of coffee from the tray Addy had put down on the counter and looked at us expectantly.

"Addy was just telling me about a group of friends staying at the inn, isn't that right, Addy?" I asked, hoping she was quick on her feet.

She nodded her head. "Oh, yes, it's a great story. There's this girl who's got the hots for one of the men. They've known each other since they were teenagers, but she's too afraid to tell him how she feels. So I told her to kiss him already."

Alex grinned. "That's a lot of details your guests tell you."

"So, Addy, did you get those papers I sent over?" I asked in a feeble attempt to change the subject. I felt my cheeks turn beetroot and I couldn't bring myself to look at Alex.

"I sure did, and it all looks fine. Oh, before I forget, how did the interview go yesterday?"

"It went great," I said. "I think it's going to be a positive article this time. Thanks again for arranging that for me, Addy."

"Sorry to interrupt, but we're getting started again," Pam said.

Addy slung her purse around her body and put her

gloves back on. "I'd best get going then. I do have one thing I wanted to ask you though."

"What's that?" I asked.

"Well, the Snow Ball is coming up fast and I don't have anything to wear. I lost a lot of weight the past year," she added in a whispered voice, as if it was a crime to have had a couple of extra pounds on her. "How would you feel about going to the big city with me tonight and doing some shopping? Just us girls. They have late-night shopping during the holidays, so it wouldn't interfere with the store's operating hours. If it's not too much trouble of course."

I smiled at her. "Not at all. It's been ages since I went on a girls' shopping trip."

Her face lit up like a Christmas tree. "Great. I'll pick you up at seven." Her curly hair peeked from under her pink wool hat and danced around her face as she left the store with a spring in her step.

"How about we open this bottle of champagne to use for the cover photo?" Pam asked. She put two crystal champagne glasses on the counter and Alex took the chilled bottle from her. He popped the cork and filled the glasses with sparkling liquid.

"To our dedication for doing this photo shoot," he said.

"To us," I answered and downed the entire glass in one take.

"You might have to rethink that," Pam said with a laugh. "The glasses are supposed to be full for the shoot."

"Oops, my mistake."

Alex refilled my glass and we took our positions to capture the cover photo. He put one hand around my waist and I put mine around his neck. I didn't know if his intense gaze was just for the photo or if it was real, but I did know one thing. This was turning out to be a very merry Christmas.

CHAPTER TWELVE

At precisely seven o'clock that evening, Addy tooted the horn of her dark blue Honda. Snowflakes swirled around in the light of the street lanterns and I pulled my coat tighter as I locked the front door.

I'd swapped the black dress and red stockings I'd worn for the photo shoot with Alex for a comfortable sweater and jeans, and tied my hair into a messy bun. I was more than ready for a night of fun.

I hadn't lied when I told Addy that it had been a long time since I'd gone on a girls' shopping trip. Even though Los Angeles was my home now, most of my friends lived far away and shopping alone just wasn't as fun as it used to be.

I walked down the path toward the car and took a quick

glance at Alex's house. The curtains were drawn, but I could still see the lights of his Christmas tree dance their now familiar rhythm. *Light. Blink, blink, blink. Light. Blink, blink.* How those flashing lights hadn't driven him crazy yet, I didn't know.

"All set?" Addy asked as I clicked my seatbelt in place.

"One hundred percent."

She pulled the car onto the snowy road. The wipers had to work overtime to clear her field of vision.

"If you open the glove compartment, you'll find some treats for our trip. I didn't know what you liked, so I bought a selection of my favorites."

I clicked the glove compartment open and several candy bars fell out. The thing was packed with candy and chocolate.

"Exactly how far away is the mall?" I asked. Judging from the amount of treats, it looked as if we had a five-hour trip in front of us.

"It's about forty-five minutes. Maybe an hour in this weather."

I grabbed a small bag filled with cookies and shut the glove compartment. The cookies smelled divine and tasted equally good.

"Cookie?" I offered. "These are delicious. You have to taste them."

"I'm good, thanks. I've tasted them a thousand times already. I made them myself."

"Wow. If I knew how to bake like this, I'd gain fifty pounds."

Addy smiled. "Every year, everyone in Old Pine Cove bakes cookies or cakes for the Snow Ball. I can teach you if you want and then you won't have to show up empty-handed."

"That's so kind of you. If I can find the time, I'd love to learn how to make these," I said. "Although I have to ask, where does everyone around here find the time? Baking cookies, organizing the Snow Ball, setting up the Christmas village in the town square, doing the Winter Walk..."

Addy shrugged. "I guess I'm just so used to it that I don't question it. Old Pine Cove has a real sense of community and we love making special occasions even more special. What's better than celebrating Christmas together, everyone pitching in, no one being left out?"

In just a couple of weeks, Addy had grown on me. Her sweet and positive personality made it easy to feel comfortable around her. I was sure that if I wasn't leaving soon, we would've become best friends.

After fifty minutes in the car, Addy pulled into the mall parking lot. The place was bustling with last-minute shoppers. There were young families pushing through the crowd, shopping bags dangling from the sides of their strollers. More than a few older couples strolled from store to store, basking in the beautifully decorated shop windows.

"Are you looking for anything in particular?" I asked Addy, trying to match her strides. The girl was on a mission.

"There's a store just around this corner where they sell the most gorgeous dresses. I've been dreaming of buying one ever since I decided I needed to lose weight," she said. "They are not cheap, but I consider it a present to myself for sticking with it. Here we are." We stopped in front of a small store, the words *Lucky Dresses No. 7* elegantly written on a sign above the entrance.

"Addy," one of the shop assistants called out. She enveloped Addy into a welcoming hug. How did this girl manage to know everything and everyone?

"Irene, this is Suzie. She's new in Old Pine Cove and she's going to help me choose a dress."

Irene greeted me with a warm smile. "I love Old Pine Cove. I used to drive all the way there for book club. Unfortunately, the book club is no longer up and running."

"Really? I'm the new store manager of the Old Pine Cove bookstore," I said.

"Well, what are the odds?" Irene said and led us toward a seating area at the back of the store. The wall was lined with floor-to-ceiling mirrors, with dressing rooms on either side. We put our purses and coats on the leather sofa that was positioned opposite the mirrors.

"I've been in here countless times before," Addy said, as if she could read my thoughts. "Irene was always kind enough to let me browse the dresses without buying anything. I didn't want to get a dress until I'd reached my goal. Minus thirty-five pounds."

"And a half," Irene said with a wink, making Addy laugh.

"True," she said.

"Are you girls up for some champagne? It's the holidays after all and this is a very special occasion for our girl here,"

Irene said.

I exchanged looks with Addy, who looked more than eager for a glass of bubbles. "Sure, why not?"

"I'll bring those around right away. Why don't you two start your tour around the store? You can pick out anything you like and try them all on. Don't be worried if a style you thought would look great on you doesn't. A dress needs to choose you as much as you choose it."

Addy and I got up and perused the store like two excited teenage girls. Everything looked amazing.

I stopped to admire the stitch work on a little black dress. It had light gray bohemian shapes delicately weaved through the fabric. On any other dress it would've looked tacky, but not on this one. I let the soft fabric slip through my fingers.

"You should try that one on," Addy said. She was standing beside me with an armful of dresses, some short, some long.

I let go of the dress. "I don't know. When would I even wear this?"

"You could wear it at the Snow Ball?"

A blush spread over my cheeks. "Actually, Alex suggested I wear the dress we used for the shoot. The photographer said I could borrow it for a couple more days if I wanted to."

"He's invited you to the Snow Ball?"

I shrugged. "It's no big deal. It could be fun, though."

"It *is* a big deal."

"Maybe." I grinned. "But you know what else is a big

deal? You buying a stunning dress. Why don't you try one on?"

Addy disappeared into one of the dressing rooms and Irene handed me a glass of ice-cold champagne with a strawberry floating at the surface.

"So, what do think of life in Old Pine Cove, Suzie?" she asked while we waited for Addy to show us the dress she was trying on. I told her how kind Addy had been to me, making me feel right at home.

"She's living next to a guy I think she should date, but she keeps saying that they're just friends. I still think there's more to it," Addy called out from the dressing room. Apparently there was no way of keeping my private life private around here either.

Irene arched an eyebrow and smiled, her interest piqued. "Do tell. I adore a good love story."

I chuckled. "There's nothing to tell. We met ten years ago when I was on vacation in Old Pine Cove. I had a crush on him and things quickly ended when I accidentally crashed his truck. We decided to try a long-distance relationship, but things didn't work out. And now he's my neighbor for the time being. It's not exciting at all. You could even say it's one hell of a boring story."

Irene laughed. "Girl, the way you blush and light up when speaking about him, I'd say it's the opposite of dull."

"That's what I've been trying to tell her," Addy shouted from behind the curtain. "But she's a stubborn one."

"I don't get why you're so obsessed with me and Alex becoming a thing," I said to Addy. "No offense."

She opened the curtain and walked toward the mirror, flattening out the creases with her hands.

"I'm not sure about this dress. What do you think?"

"Maybe try one of the others. It's not a hell yeah for me."

She turned around, disappearing behind the curtain again. "And Alex? Is he a hell yeah?"

"What?"

"I'm sorry, I'm pushy, right? It's just… I've been hurt before, just like Alex, and it shook me up big time. So when I see that two people share a connection, a spark even, I get excited. Because to me, love needs to win. Love is the only cure for having had your heart broken. Love is… life. Seeing you and Alex together gives me hope. Hope that I too will be able to love someone again someday. My gosh, it sounds so silly and dramatic when I say it out loud, doesn't it?"

"It doesn't," I said. "I had no idea you've been through a heart-wrenching breakup like that."

"It's okay, Suzie. And in a way you're right. I shouldn't meddle like this."

Irene turned to me and put a hand on my leg. "In all honesty, though, do you like this guy? Could you see whatever is going on between you two blossoming into something more? Because if there's something I've learned from watching people come in here and listening to their stories all these years, it's that you should always follow your heart."

I sighed. "The thing is, I don't know what my heart

wants. How does anyone? How can you trust an act so irrational as opening yourself up to someone?"

I didn't want to tell them I'd never been in a serious relationship before. At least not one that lasted longer than a couple of months and where I got to introduce the guy to my family.

"It's about diving into the deep end with your eyes closed, I guess. You expect the best, but also brace yourself for impact. Living it is the only way to discover if it was the right choice."

I mulled over Irene's words for a moment. When Alex and I talked, I often felt that familiar feeling of joy that I'd felt ten years ago. But that was just because I used to have a crush on him and my subconscious mind still associated him with those feelings, no?

A shiver went through me when I presented myself with the thought of Irene and Addy being right all along. Maybe there *was* something more between us. More than I'd dared to admit. Did I… have genuine feelings for Alex that I should pursue?

Even if that was true, there were still risks involved. If I gave up my life in L.A. for him and things didn't work out between us, then what? I would have nowhere to go. I couldn't imagine staying in Old Pine Cove if Alex broke my heart. But my L.A. job wouldn't be there for me to return to either. I didn't know if I was willing to take those risks.

"I'm coming out again," Addy said, jolting me out of my reverie. She shoved the curtain open and twirled in front of the mirror. "What do you think?"

The dress she was wearing reached all the way to the floor, the soft pink chiffon falling elegantly around her legs. The sleeveless top was embellished with tiny rhinestones and a small sash sat snug around her waist.

"This is the one," I said. "This is the dress."

Irene nodded, a delighted look on her face. "She's right. You look stunning."

"I almost feel like I've found the perfect wedding dress," Addy said with a giggle.

"This calls for more champagne, right, girls?" Irene topped up everyone's glasses. "To finding dresses... and love."

***

"So, what do you see?" I asked.

Addy turned the cup around in her hands and inspected its contents. She'd offered to buy me a drink and read my tea leaves after her successful dress hunt. I'd gladly accepted. Even though I didn't believe in that kind of thing, it sounded like a fun thing to do.

"Hmm," she said. "Yes, yes."

"Do you see anything?" I asked, peering into the cup as well.

"It says love is waiting for you. But the decision is up to you."

I snorted. "You just made that up, didn't you?"

"I did not. My mother was a fantastic tea leaf reader

and taught me everything I know. All of this is true."

"So what else do you see?"

"Success in your career. Yes, definitely," she said, nodding. "Some great things are waiting for you."

I let out a laugh. "I'm glad it all sounds positive. Thank you."

Addy put the cup down. "This was a lot of fun, Suzie. Thank you for coming with me."

"Thanks for inviting me. I had a great time. I can't wait to see you in that dress at the Snow Ball. You're going to be the star of the night, no doubt about it."

"What do you say about eating some more of those cookies on the way back home?"

"I'd love that," I said.

We linked arms as we walked back to the car. The air was chilly. I shivered. I didn't know if I'd ever get used to the cold, but it sure was beautiful up here. It had stopped snowing and the sky had cleared again. I looked up at the infinite amount of stars shining down on us. This kind of thing seemed impossible in L.A. There was always too much light around to get a clear view of the night sky.

"You're going to find your magic, you know," Addy said as we reached the car.

As we got in, I wondered if she was right, or if I'd already found it and was too stubborn to realize it. I guessed there was only one way of finding out: diving into the deep end, both eyes closed and bracing myself for impact.

CHAPTER THIRTEEN

With a busy and exciting day ahead, I got up earlier than usual so I wouldn't have to stress about getting ready on time. Becca Loveheart was arriving and I wanted everything to be perfect. She was coming over later today to get familiarized with the setting and do a test reading of the story she was going to read for the Winter Walk. After that, she'd return to the inn until the big event tomorrow.

I'd spent the entire previous day prepping the store for the Winter Walk. Alex had told me that they had two hundred and fifty tickets every year, but most years only sold about a hundred. Even a hundred seemed like a lot to handle, but Alex promised that people wouldn't come into the store all at once, as there were several stops and starting points along the way.

The coffee machine filled the house with that addictive coffee scent while I took a hot shower. I slipped on a knee-length dress and blow-dried my hair before heading to the kitchen. With a mug of hot coffee, I sat myself down at the table and looked outside to the snowy street. Sunlight filtered through the trees and made the snow look like it was infused with glitter. I could understand why people loved spending the holidays in Old Pine Cove. This kind of peace and quiet was hard to find in a big city.

My mobile phone came to life and I looked at the screen before answering.

"Morning, Kate."

"Hi, Suzie. How's everything going for the signing? Has Becca arrived yet? Or someone from the press?"

"Not yet, although the inn's owner told me she arrived perfectly safe yesterday evening and they gave her their best room. I'm meeting Becca this afternoon to go over the details."

"Good. Remember to give her everything she needs. Now, I have some good news for you. We might've found a candidate to take over the store. We still have to evaluate her further of course, but she looks solid on paper. She even lived in Old Pine Cove at one point. I guess you'll be able to leave sometime next week and spend New Year's in L.A."

"Wow, really?"

"It's great, right? I'll keep you updated on any progress. We can't wait to have you back here."

"And the store manager position? Someone told me that the board insisted on having job interviews?"

"That's true, but you've got some extra experience under your belt now. That'll skew things in your favor for sure. Why don't we discuss the details when you get back?"

"Sure, that sounds good to me."

"Great. Have a fantastic day, Suzie."

I hung up the phone and pressed my lips together. So it was official. Well, almost. I would be leaving this place next week and diving right back into my familiar L.A. life.

I fired off a message to Dean, telling him we'd be reunited soon, and he replied with a bunch of party emoticons. But for some reason, I couldn't muster up the same enthusiasm. What was wrong with me? Why wasn't I jumping for joy to get back to my life?

A knock on the door sent a sliver of panic through me. Was Becca here already? I checked the time on my phone. She wasn't due to arrive for another five hours and I still had to prepare some things.

But instead of Becca, I found Alex standing before me.

"Morning," he said.

"Morning, Alex. Come on in."

"I won't stay long," he said, stepping inside. "I just wanted to ask if you'd like to help me pick up the snow globes from the factory later."

"You want me to help you with those? I mean, I'd be happy to, but I don't know if I'm the best choice of person to accompany you there."

He laughed. "I won't let you drive of course. These

snow globes all need to arrive in one piece."

"Aren't you funny," I said. "But yes, I'll help."

"Also, I wanted to give you this." He handed me a copy of *Old Pine Cove Weekly*. "It's got a new article about you, only this time it's positive."

"Well, thank you," I said, clutching the paper under my arm like an old man.

"Are you nervous?"

"About the paper?"

Alex grinned. "About the Winter Walk. You haven't heard?"

I racked my brain for some vital piece of information I was clearly missing, but I couldn't figure out what it was.

"We're completely sold out. This has never happened in the fifteen years we've been organizing the Winter Walk. I think your author event might have something to do with it."

"Sold out?"

"We're trying to see if we can accommodate more people. There's a waitlist and everything. Everyone's so excited. Georgia and Delilah are even baking extra cakes so that there'll be enough for everyone. The whole town is bustling with excitement and it's mostly because of your great ideas."

"That's amazing. Although I'm not sure I can take all the credit. Becca Loveheart was going to do a signing anyway, regardless of the Winter Walk."

"But you came up with the theme and tied it to the signing. It was genius."

"I wasn't nervous before, but I sure am now," I said with a laugh.

"Well, I'll be off then. I'll see you tonight. Call me if you need any additional help."

I looked around the bookstore. Where was I going to fit all these people? The store wasn't big enough to host a more than sold-out event.

"I might take you up on that offer. We need to rethink the seating, the placement of the food tables, the acoustics."

"Tell you what, I'll come back later today and help you. That way, you won't have to stress out about it and you can focus on making that author feel right at home in our town. Leave the details and logistics to me."

"You're a lifesaver," I said and pulled him into a tight hug. My sudden move made it clear that I was delirious from the news he had just given me.

I let go of Alex and he shot me a roguish grin. "There is one other thing we have to settle. It's about the Snow Ball."

"Yes?"

"Since my girlfriend ran away last year and you're here all alone… Well, we can't show up at the Snow Ball as two lonely people, right? I feel like we should stick together." He paused for a moment and then continued. "Suzie Stonebrooks, do you want to be my official date to the Snow Ball tomorrow?"

A fluttering feeling made its way through my belly. I didn't get asked on dates a lot, especially not by a hottie like Alex. "I would love to be your date."

"Good," he said, and he walked out of the door.

My excitement was too big to be contained, so I ran upstairs and did a little living room happy dance.

Things were looking up. Better yet, things were looking extremely bright. The sold-out event might've been an unimpressive achievement if it had taken place in our L.A. store, but it meant a lot for a small branch in Old Pine Cove, especially this close to Christmas. Kate would love it.

And then I'd also scored a date with Alex. He had suggested going together before of course, but it wasn't official up until now. The familiar mixture of fear and excitement swirled through me. I let out a nervous laugh. I was going to go to the Snow Ball with the most handsome man in town. It sounded unbelievable, yet it was true. I would have a fairytale night before heading back to Los Angeles next week, and I just couldn't wait to savor every fleeting moment.

***

"And this is where you can sign the books. We'll make sure people form a proper queue and there will be someone to keep an eye on how long they spend talking to you. We were thinking two minutes per person, tops."

Becca Loveheart nodded and smiled. "That all sounds perfect to me."

Addy had dropped her off at the store half an hour ago. My hands kept shaking and my voice came out all high-pitched, but I hoped Becca was happy with what she saw.

"Do you have any additional questions?"

"I do. Where do you keep the wine and can we have a glass right now?"

"Sure we can. Why don't you go upstairs and I'll be right back with the wine," I said, showing her the way to the living room. I dashed out of the front door and ran over to Alex's place, hoping he'd have a bottle of wine lying around.

"Do you have any appetizers to serve with the wine?" he asked, taking a bottle out of the fridge.

"If a half-eaten packet of chocolate chip cookies and a bag of cereal counts as appetizers, then yes, I do. Oh, and I've also got a dozen cups of instant noodles."

Alex frowned. "I can't tell whether you're joking or whether you're telling the truth."

"It's the truth."

"Suzie, you can't serve that woman a bowl of instant noodles. Why don't you take this bottle back to your place and I'll whip something up? I'll be there in about fifteen minutes."

"You would do that for me?"

He shrugged. "Why wouldn't I? It's no hassle and I can't let you feed cereal and wine to the star of the Winter Walk."

"I appreciate that. Thank you. You can use your spare key, just come on up."

"I will. Oh, and I'll charge you later," he said with a wink, then started rummaging through his cupboards.

I hurried back and joined Becca in the living room with two full wine glasses.

"Cheers," she said. She downed half the glass in one go. "I needed this. Traveling can be stressful, don't you think? Sometimes you just want to kick back and enjoy some wine."

"Totally," I said. It felt weird sharing a glass of wine with someone so popular, and whom I looked up to.

"I loved your latest book," I said, breaking the silence between us.

"Aw, thank you. I'm always extremely nervous before a new release. You never know if people are going to love it or hate it, and when you work so hard on something… Well, it's enough to drive a woman to drink."

"You've got nothing to be nervous about," I said. "You're one of the most talented writers I know."

She laughed. "That's kind of you to say, but believe me, I'm not perfect. I do know that I'm a lot better than when I first started this career, but I guess that's how it always goes. Practice makes perfect. And with fifteen books under my belt, I know just how to hit those bestseller charts."

"Being an author sounds amazing, but I don't know if I'd be able to pull it off."

"Nonsense, why wouldn't you? I get that it's scary, but if you want to achieve something, you have no choice but to put yourself out there. Do you write?"

"I do, but I'm afraid of people hating my work."

"Oh, you'll get negative feedback for sure. Everyone does. Your style won't be for everyone and people can be harsh, especially online. But if you never try, you'll never know what it would've been like to reach your dreams."

"Kind of like love," I said.

"A lot like love, yes. You can't get someone to love you if you don't open yourself up to them, even though being vulnerable is hard and scary. It's the same with writing."

The bell of the store jingled and I sprang to my feet. "That'll be Alex, my neighbor."

"Knock, knock," he called out, and stepped into the living room with a platter filled with cheese, grapes, olives, some bread and an assortment of nuts.

"That looks delicious," Becca said as he set the platter on the coffee table. "Much better than those soggy sandwiches they often have at events."

"Becca's right, this looks amazing. Thanks so much."

"It's no biggie. You ladies enjoy," he said and then turned to me. "How about I start rearranging some things downstairs to fit everyone in? And then we'll head to the factory around six?"

"Perfect," I said and closed the door behind him.

Becca raised her eyebrows. "That hottie is your neighbor? I wonder how you get any sleep at night knowing he's only a few feet away from you."

I let out a high-pitched laugh. "Oh, we're just friends."

She ignored my comment. "If he's as skilled in the bedroom as he is in the kitchen, well... you're in for a treat, girl.

I shrugged and put a piece of cheese in my mouth so I wouldn't have to say anything. Not that I didn't want to, but admitting how I felt to Becca would mean admitting it out loud once and for all and I didn't know if I could handle that.

CHAPTER FOURTEEN

The snow globe factory was located just outside of the town center and employed thirty-eight people. They didn't only make themed and personalized snow globes, but also offered tours of the factory and had a small snow globe museum. At least, that was the intel Alex gave me on the drive there.

"Hey, Karen. We're here to pick up the charity boxes," Alex told the lady at the reception. Her plump face lit up at the sight of him.

"Alex, how good to see you. How are you? Oh, and who is your guest?" she asked with a twinkle in her eye.

"This is Suzie. She's running the bookstore for a while."

"It's great to meet you, dear. How long will you be in Old Pine Cove?"

"I don't know yet," I lied. "Until they find someone to take over the store permanently."

I hadn't broken the news about my impending departure to Alex yet and this didn't seem like the best situation to do it. I'd tell him as soon as we were alone.

"Well, while you're here, why don't you take the factory tour? We've got one starting in thirty minutes. It's on the house," she said.

Alex ran a hand through his hair and shot me a sideways glance. "I don't know if Suzie has the time right now."

"Nonsense," I said. "Last time I was here, I didn't get the chance to do the tour. I'd love to."

Alex grinned. "I guess you can put us on the list for the next tour then, Karen. Could you please tell Donald I'll pick up the boxes after the tour?"

"Very well." She handed us two tickets. "Enjoy," she said and picked up the phone to call Donald about the change of plans.

"Let's check out the museum while we wait for the tour to start," I said.

Alex led me through a hallway on the right. The ceiling had Christmas baubles dangling from it, all positioned at different heights. We entered a brightly lit lobby area which had an arched doorway leading to the museum.

"After you," Alex said.

I stepped inside. Row upon row upon row of snow globes lined the walls. A small carpeted walkway snaked across the room into another one.

I stepped over to one of the glass cases.

"Look, this explains how snow globes were invented," I said. I scanned the text in front of me. "Apparently they've been around since the nineteenth century and were patented in 1900."

As I followed the snaking pathway and learned more about the history of snow globes, I started to understand why people found this factory so appealing. It was as if they had perfected the art of snow globe making.

"These snow globes were all designed manually. Can you believe that?" I said, pointing to a large case filled with the most detailed snow globes I'd ever seen. "The factory here only started using machines in the nineties and even now there's still a team of people who manually paint certain parts. Isn't that amazing?"

I walked toward the next case, which was filled with personalized snow globes. "I think I'm going to order one of these. How cool would that be?"

Alex said nothing, but threw me a smile that made my knees buckle.

"What?" I asked.

"You're adorable, getting all excited about snow globes."

"I am not," I said, laughing.

"You are. The fact that you don't realize it makes you even more adorable."

I put my hand on my hip. "I'm sure you say that to all the girls."

Alex took a step forward and locked eyes with me. He stood so close that I could smell his shampoo. Honey and lime, a strange yet scintillating combination of fragrances.

He brushed a strand of hair out of my face and a shiver ran through me.

"You're the first girl I've ever brought back here," he whispered.

I swallowed. It was like his hands and his words had set my skin on fire and I had no way of extinguishing these raging flames. All I could think of were his lips only inches away from mine. A stark contrast with the physical distance between us in real life.

"Okay." It was all I managed to say. Forming a full sentence seemed impossible.

"You're not only adorable, but the most beautiful girl I've ever seen. I knew it ten years ago and I know it now."

He raised his left hand and traced the outline of my bottom lip with his finger. He was making me all shaky. I had to react, show him how much I wanted him to kiss me. Without thinking things through, I bit his finger.

"Ah, here you two are. The tour's about to start," I heard a woman's voice say.

I immediately took a step back as if I'd gotten stung by a bee. The world was starting to come into focus again. I put my hands deep into my pockets and prayed that Karen hadn't seen me biting Alex's finger.

"Thanks, we'll be right there, Karen," Alex said, his face flushing.

"Take your time," she said with a wink before heading back to the reception desk.

"I guess we'd better go then," Alex said. "Although I do feel bad about getting interrupted like that."

"Me too," I said, locking eyes with him. His smile set my body alight.

I followed Alex out of the room and we joined a group of seven others, all of them tourists. There was a couple from France, a family of four from Denver and a middle-aged man who told us his wife had to cancel the tour because she'd contracted a tummy bug. According to him, it was pretty nasty and she hadn't left the toilet in over two hours. Not exactly information I was dying to know.

Alex introduced us, yet didn't say a word about how we knew each other. As I followed the group onto the factory floor, I wondered what our connection even was. Every now and then I took small glances at him. Was he feeling as confused as I was? Why on earth had I bitten his finger as if I was a vampire?

Alex showed no signs of confusion, though. He nodded at the exact right times and laughed at everyone's jokes. I on the other hand didn't register a thing the tour guide was saying. If there was a test at the end, I'd fail for sure.

"And here we have our *pièce de résistance*," the tour guide said, snapping me out of my thoughts.

All kinds of *oohs* and *aahs* went through the group as we gathered around the most gigantic snow globe I'd ever seen. It was twice my size, and inside was a very accurate depiction of the Old Pine Cove Santa's Village I had visited with Alex last week.

"You are all free to take a picture here."

"*Merveilleux*," the French couple said and asked the guide to snap their picture. They hugged the snow globe, one on each side.

"You want one as well?" Alex asked.

I looked at the family of four. They were pretending to push the snow globe and had everyone in laughing fits, even though it wasn't that funny to witness. Their enthusiasm was adorable though.

"Oh, I don't know," I said. A silly picture with a giant snow globe wasn't on my wish list, but Alex ignored me. He handed the French guy his phone and strolled over to the globe.

"Come on, I won't bite," he called out to me, and pulled me next to him. "Biting is more your thing anyway," he said, making my cheeks crank up the heat.

"Just a leeeetlle closer," the French guy said, waiting for us to huddle together as if we were a real couple.

Alex put his arm around my shoulders and gave me a small squeeze. Maybe I hadn't been wrong after all. Maybe he loved vampires. Or maybe I was just crazy for thinking any of it had been a good idea.

"Last stop is the gift shop, everyone. Through here," the tour guide said.

"Do you mind meeting me out front in fifteen?" Alex asked me. "I've got to track down Donald to load the snow globes for the charity onto my truck."

"Sure. I mean, I have no choice, do I? You drove me here," I said, smiling.

Alex let out a chuckle. "That's one way of looking at it."

We parted ways and I ventured into the gift shop. There was a section with snow globes depicting all the town's buildings, like Dave's Diner, and the town square with its big Christmas tree. They would make perfect gifts for my friends and family back home.

I browsed through the items and decided on a snow globe with a reindeer pulling a sleigh for my parents and a snow-globe-shaped mug for Dean that said "Don't shake me".

Should I get Alex something? As I walked from shelf to shelf, not finding anything special enough to gift him, I worried that maybe I didn't know him that well. Then again, how could I? I had only been living in Old Pine Cove for a few weeks. That was hardly enough time to get to know someone well enough to make an informed decision about what to buy them, right?

Still, we had spent a lot of time together. I forced myself to think about Alex long and hard. I knew he loved yoga. That he was a great chef. That he was a neat freak. That he'd never say no to a day at the ski slopes and that he was the kind of guy who'd always help someone in need, even though his sometimes tough demeanor suggested otherwise.

As I was waiting in line at the cashier's desk, a medium-sized snow globe caught my eye. It had a detailed scene of a smiling person flipping pancakes. The globe was positioned on top of a restaurant all decked out in Christmas décor. It was perfect and it screamed Alex.

A smile spread across my face as the cashier gift-wrapped the snow globe. I *did* know Alex. So why did I want to let myself believe we were strangers who had nothing more to give to each other than a few weeks of neighborly friendliness?

I thought back to what Becca had told me earlier that day. She'd made me realize that sometimes we're so afraid of winning, we'd rather let ourselves believe losing is better. But it never is.

I sat down in the waiting area. Was I being led by fear? Should I open myself up to… love? I winced. How did people do it? How did they let themselves go past the point of no return? To the land of vulnerability where the likelihood of getting your heart broken was sky high?

"A penny for your thoughts."

Alex seemed to have materialized out of nowhere. His hair was peeking out from under his wool hat and he gave me the kind of smile that erased every last shred of doubt I had. What he stirred up inside of me was something I had never felt before. I was falling for him and there was no stopping this train of feelings. It had left the station, loud and clear.

"I was just thinking about snow globes," I said, which wasn't a complete lie.

"I've got a truck full of them. Although, I have to say that I'm nervous about having you on board as well."

"Oh?" I said.

"You don't have the best track record with the snow globe and truck combo."

I gave him a playful push. "Oh, shut up. You know what? If it eases your nerves, I'll walk."

He gently grabbed me by the arm and pulled me toward

him. "Don't be silly. We're in this together. I guess it's our history that's making me feel this nervous."

I swallowed. "I know how that feels."

"Fear has a strange way of sneaking up on people, right?"

"Are you afraid that we'll crash and burn? The truck I mean."

"You have no idea."

"The way I see it, there's only one option. We commit to the ride and we'll see where we end up. It doesn't have to be a disaster."

Alex nodded, our fingers intertwining. "You're right. It could be smooth sailing."

"The snow globes could all arrive in one piece. As long as we take extra special care of them."

"I want to take care of them so badly," he whispered. "I want to make sure they feel cherished and loved."

I nodded. "Yes, please."

He looked at me, his dark eyes full of desire.

A faint ringing sound broke the magic moment like a popping balloon. I tried to ignore it, but whoever was calling wasn't planning on stopping any time soon.

"I think your phone is ringing," I said.

He put a hand on my cheek, the tip of his strong thumb grazing my skin. "Let it ring."

The ringing stopped and I smiled. Finally.

"Now it's you," Alex said with a laugh. "Can't anyone leave us alone for two minutes?"

I got my phone out of my bag and looked at the screen.

"It's Addy."

Alex took his phone out of his pocket and frowned. "She tried calling me as well."

"I'd better pick up then. It might be urgent." A feeling of unease filled my stomach. Why was Addy calling me at this hour?

I accepted the call with trembling hands. "Hey, Addy. Is everything okay?"

"Something has happened to the store. I was here to drop off the last two cakes for the Winter Walk tomorrow and I wanted to use the spare key you gave me, but when I approached the front door, it was wide open and, and, well—"

"Slow down, what's wrong?"

"I think you'd better come down here," she said. "You have to see this to believe it."

CHAPTER FIFTEEN

"I'm so sorry, Suzie."

Addy was holding the door open for me and threw me a pained look. Alex and I had raced over to the store as fast as we could without endangering the delicate load of snow globes in the back.

"Don't be. None of this is your fault. If anything, I'm lucky that you noticed before things got even more out of control. I don't understand why someone would do this, though."

The current state of the store brought tears to my eyes. The seven cakes that Addy had brought over earlier for the Winter Walk were all ruined. I had left them on the counter, each in an airtight plastic container, thinking nothing could happen to them while I was away with Alex. It's not like I left a box of gold out in the open. Plus, this was Old Pine Cove. The town wasn't exactly known for its high crime rates.

Each cake had been smashed to pieces. Big chunks of cake and crumbs were spread out over the floor and over an entire table full of Becca Loveheart's books. I couldn't sell those anymore, let alone have them signed.

The plastic containers lay open on the floor, next to my Christmas tree. Or at least, what was left of it. It looked like the tree had exploded, sending shards of broken baubles in all possible directions.

And then there were the ten milk cartons we were going to use for the signing. We'd promised everyone a free cup of hot cocoa. All the cartons been cut open and stomped on, causing the milk to go into every nook and cranny.

How was I going to explain this to Kate? And what about the book signing and the Winter Walk? People would be arriving in less than twenty-four hours. I couldn't possibly ask customers to make their way through aisles filled with glass, milk and cake crumbs, now could I? My stomach churned at the thought of cancelling everything.

"What kind of person would do something like this?" I repeated, more to myself than to the others.

"The kind that hates cake," Alex said. "And Christmas."

"Or me," I said, trying to fight back the tears I could feel pushing their way through. "Christmas is ruined."

Addy shook her head. "Oh no, it isn't."

"But look at... this! All the cakes everyone put so much love and energy into are smashed to pieces by someone who's got to have an arm like a wrecking ball. What am I going to tell the people who signed up for the Winter Walk?"

Alex picked up one of the containers and put it on the counter. "Addy's right, you know. It's not ruined until it's over. We still have, what, about twenty hours to make things right again? That's plenty of time to fix this. We'll both help you, right Addy?"

"Of course," Addy replied. "That's what friends are for."

"I'd be more than happy to bake new cakes," Alex said. "I'll also make a call to the police department, ask if they can go around the neighborhood. Maybe some of the neighbors saw some unusual activity tonight that can lead us to the person responsible for this."

"And I can help you clean this mess up, Suzie," Addy said. "Oh, and we should take some pictures for insurance purposes."

Alex nodded. "Good thinking. What do you say, Suzie?"

"I don't know, it's late and I don't want to be a burden. Don't you have to get back to the inn?" I asked Addy.

"My staff's covering for me."

"And you're not a burden," Alex said. "This is standard town policy. We help each other out, no matter what."

I plastered on a smile. "Well, I can't go against town policy now can I?"

"That's the spirit," Addy said. "Now, where do you keep the garbage bags?"

***

Three hours and several full garbage bags later, Addy and I had managed to get the entire store back to an acceptable state. I had vacuumed everything twice, to make sure not one shard of glass got left behind. The milk had been mopped up and I'd scrubbed the floors. I could only hope there wouldn't be too many stains left after everything had dried.

After throwing out the last unsalvageable copies of Becca's books, I'd sent Addy home so she could sleep. I was exhausted as well, but still needed to redecorate my Christmas tree.

As I swept up the last shards of baubles from around the tree Addy and I had put back up, I noticed a piece of jewelry amongst the glass. I carefully pulled it out. A small feather earring rested in the palm of my hand. One of my customers had probably lost it while browsing through books. I decided to put it behind the counter so that I would be able to easily locate it if and when the rightful owner showed up to claim it.

I looked around the store and felt a sense of relief wash over me. Nothing gave away the fact that Got It Covered had been trashed by an insane person, apart from the still drying floor. I did lose a lot of stock, but at least I wouldn't have to cancel the signing.

A short knock on the door startled me.

"Hey, Hollywood."

"Hey, Doug," I said, letting the police officer in. "Nice

to see you again. Although I'd love for the circumstances to be different."

"That's what everyone always says," he replied with a smile. "I went to talk with your neighbors, but most of them were at the community center, working on the decorations for the Snow Ball."

"So you didn't find out anything," I said.

Doug shook his head. "I'm sorry, love. But don't worry. That doesn't mean this case can't be solved."

"Thanks anyway. I appreciate you taking the time to help me."

He let out a loud laugh. "Of course, it's my job after all. Speaking of which, why don't we go through the house together and check all the weak points in your security?"

"Sure." We investigated every window and door in the house, after which Doug told me that it would be best to put extra locks on all of them and maybe have some of the windows replaced entirely, as they were easy to break.

"Look," he said then, while pointing at the back door. It was slightly ajar. "This is definitely how the culprit was able to get into the store. The door is so old that anyone could push it open."

"I'll make sure to share all of this information with the owners so that they can fix the security issues around the place," I said. "I don't know if I'll feel safe sleeping here tonight, though."

"Tell you what, I'll put a sliding lock on the back door for you. That way you'll be safe until the door gets replaced."

I walked to the counter and handed Doug the earring I'd found earlier. "I did find this on the floor. Maybe it could lead to a tip?"

Doug put the earring in his coat pocket. "Tell you what, I'll have Hugo write an article about it. There's a special Christmas issue of *Old Pine Weekly* releasing tomorrow. I'm sure he can fit it in somewhere."

"Thanks so much, Doug."

"No worries. I want to find this perp as much as you."

By the time Doug left, all I wanted was to get some sleep, but I still had to redecorate my Christmas tree. Without any leftover decorations, that would be hard.

I pulled my coat on and went next door to Alex's house. Maybe he had an extra set of baubles stacked somewhere that I could use.

His front door swung open and an involuntary chuckle escaped from my mouth. Alex was standing in the doorway wearing an apron with pictures of dancing reindeer on it. He was holding a big mixing bowl in his arms, as if he was a housewife from the fifties.

"Wow, you look… different," I said.

"If you tell me I look like an old lady, I'll have to wrestle you to the ground," he said with a grin.

I held up my hands. "You won't hear a peep out of me. Grandma," I added.

He put the bowl on the floor in the hallway and pulled me inside. "That's it. You asked for it."

I tried to make a run for the kitchen, but he grabbed me from behind and kept me in a tight hold.

"Stop," I yelled, thick tears of laughter running down my face.

"Not until you tell me I don't look like an old lady."

I tried squirming out of his strong embrace, but there was no escaping his arms. We both fell down on the hallway floor, Alex's eyes locking with mine.

"Think you can win this one, do you?" he asked.

This was my chance.

I reached my arm out, gripped the bowl of cake batter with my fingertips and pulled it toward me. Then I scooped a big blob out and smeared it all over his face.

The shocked expression on his face vanished as quickly as it had appeared, and he shot me a mischievous grin. He pinned my arms down with his hands and lowered his face. We were only inches apart. I searched his eyes, wanting to know what he was planning.

"Are you sure you're ready for this?" he asked, licking his lips.

I nodded.

"Don't say you didn't ask for it," he said and lowered his face even further. But instead of kissing me, he rubbed his nose and cheeks against mine, smearing the batter all over my face.

I grabbed a fresh handful, aiming for his neck, only for the batter to land in his hair. He took revenge by doing the same to me. The sweet smell of cake batter filled the air around us.

I grabbed the wooden spoon and held it in front of me. "I surrender. No more wrestling and no more food fights."

But Alex didn't speak. He just stared into my eyes, still pinning me in place. I met his gaze, then watched him as his eyes turned their attention to my lips.

"Also," I said. "Who's going to clean these floors?"

His breathing had turned heavier, more urgent. "Cleaning? That's what you're thinking about right now?"

"What are you thinking about then?" I asked, meeting his eyes once again.

"This," he answered.

He put one hand on my cheek and tucked my hair behind my ear. His breathing made my skin crackle with electricity, filling every part of my body with a longing desire. He let his gaze run over my face while his fingers softly caressed my neck, my ear lobes, my lips.

A short moan traveled from my insides to my mouth, until it escaped and amplified Alex's urgency. He pressed his lips onto mine and kissed them in the slowest way possible. His mouth was even softer than I'd ever imagined and his warmth radiated through me.

I tangled my fingers in his hair and pulled him even closer, wanting more. A rainbow of pure joy made my heart explode, seeping deep into my veins.

As he deepened our kiss, he erased every inch of doubt I'd had about his feelings for me. I didn't know what was going to happen now that I'd crossed that scary threshold of opening up to him, but I did know this: nothing had ever felt more right to me than this.

We came up for air, both panting, our eyes still locked on each other. I had never been kissed like that before. I would replay this moment over and over again in my mind for years to come.

"I'll have to redo that one," Alex said with a grin, pointing to the bowl on the ground, now only half full with batter.

"And to think that I only came over here to ask you about Christmas decorations," I said.

"I'm glad you did though. At first I thought you were going to stay true to your words."

"What words?"

"Dear Alex, I don't know how to say this in a friendly way. I never want to see you again and I'm never returning to Old Pine Cove either."

My cheeks turned red as he cited the first lines of the letter I'd sent him ten years ago. I had told him that I was about to start college soon and that I didn't want any distractions. There was even a line in there about wanting to be free to date other people. Gosh, just thinking about that letter made me cringe.

"In my defense, I was seventeen when I wrote that and I only said it because I was embarrassed about crashing your truck."

"Running away is never the best option, Suzie," he said. I nodded. "I know."

"Good. Now, let's get you those decorations, shall we?"

He pulled me up and led me through the hallway to his storage room, all the while holding my hand in his. Despite the disaster that had gone down at the store earlier, I couldn't help but smile.

CHAPTER SIXTEEN

I t was a little past four a.m. when I crawled into bed. I set my alarm for nine and turned off the light, but sleep didn't come, no matter how exhausted I was.

That wasn't a surprise though. This wasn't just any regular night. It was the night I had kissed Alex. Over and over again, while whisking egg whites, waiting for the cakes to rise, kneading dough into tiny balls and cutting the thick paste into cookies.

I smiled in the dark, the taste of Alex's kisses still lingering on my lips.

How was I supposed to sleep when my heart was bursting with joy? I grabbed my phone from the nightstand and opened the message app. My fingers hovered over the keyboard.

"I had fun tonight," I typed. Then I spent seven minutes adding and deleting a kiss emoji, until I decided to send the message without any bells and whistles.

The message got read right away, clueing me in on the fact that he was also far too excited to sleep.

I waited for his reply with the patience of a child waiting for Santa. Three blue dots kept dancing their steady rhythm on my screen, taunting me, driving me crazy. What on earth was he typing? A poem to let me know how much he'd enjoyed our night together?

Then the sound of a new message notification filled the room and I read his reply.

"Me too."

It wasn't a poem, yet those two words made me bite my duvet. Alex had a knack for driving me crazy.

I pressed my phone against my chest. Deep down I was afraid of what would happen now and how we would be able to turn this into something stable with thousands of miles between us, but those were worries for later. Right then and there, I wanted to pretend as if nothing stood between us. Savoring the moment had never felt so good.

***

After less than five hours of sleep, I woke up with a warm feeling in my chest, ready to rock the day. The memory of kissing Alex the night before was more than enough to energize me. I wondered if he was thinking of me while he was making breakfast. Or maybe he was still asleep, dreaming about the two of us. I shook my head. There was no time to think about these things. I had to start preparing the book signing and make sure everything was ready for the Winter Walk later that evening.

At lunchtime I headed out to grab something to eat from Dave's Diner before picking Becca Loveheart up from the inn.

I walked past the inflatable Santa positioned next to the door and almost stopped in my tracks when I saw Alex at the counter. He was talking to a wheelchair-bound Diane, who'd presumably been released from the hospital earlier than expected.

"Hello there." It was all I managed to say.

Diane arched an eyebrow, but didn't say anything. Alex on the other hand seemed oblivious to Diane's sparse friendliness towards me and pulled me into a hug.

"Diane made it back in time for the Winter Walk. Isn't that great?"

"It is," I said, even though I would have preferred to not have to deal with her meddling and judging. I had enough on my plate already.

"Maybe I'll see you at the book signing event at Got It Covered this afternoon?" I said. "Becca Loveheart is doing a reading of her latest romance novel."

Diane scoffed. "I don't read those cheap kissing books, sorry. I prefer something... more classy. Like Dickens or Jane Austen."

An awkward silence filled the space between us.

"So how come you haven't returned to L.A. yet? I

thought you were only here temporarily?"

"They still haven't found anyone to take over the store," Alex answered. "Isn't that right, Suzie?"

"They're working on it," I lied.

I hadn't told Alex yet that I'd be leaving soon. Very soon. On some level that might've been wrong of me, but he knew from the start that it was never my intention to stay in Old Pine Cove forever.

The doubt started inching its way toward my throat. If I knew we had no future, then why did I let him kiss me? Why hadn't I listened to my head instead of my heart?

"Maybe they won't find anyone for weeks. I wouldn't mind though," Alex said with a smile.

"Maybe they'll find someone sooner than we expect. Who knows, they could be interviewing someone as we speak," Diane said, then wheeled herself toward one of the empty booths.

I turned to Alex. "Are you still convinced that Diane likes me?"

He raked a hand through his hair, as if he needed time to find the right words. "That certainly was odd. But then again, who knows what's in that post-surgery medication she's taking?"

I laughed. "Yeah, you might be onto something."

"Do you want to order and walk home together?" Alex asked.

"I would love to, but I have to pick up Becca Loveheart from the inn. I do have ten minutes to spare, though. We could wait for our order together?"

"Perfect."

We both ordered a grilled cheese sandwich before slipping into the seats of an empty booth. It was the same one we'd shared the first time we went to Dave's Diner together. Outside it started to snow, covering the road in a fresh layer of white flakes. The lights of the Christmas tree in the town square were lit, even though the daylight took away some of their effect. Still, it was a beautiful sight.

"Thanks again for helping me bake those cakes," I said. "The whole thing would've been a disaster if it weren't for you. And they taste so good. Whenever I try to bake a cake, it's always way too dry."

"Well, that's easy to fix."

"I knew there was a secret I was missing all this time. Please share it with me."

Alex leaned in and whispered, "If you want your cake to taste less dry, just drink more water when eating it. Easy, right?"

I flicked his forehead. "Ha, ha, very funny, Mister Smartypants."

He pretended to be shocked. "Did you just flick me? You do remember what happened the last time you made fun of me, right?" he asked.

I grinned. "Crystal clear. Maybe that's why I flicked you."

He briefly caressed the tops of my fingers.

"About me leaving—" I started, but he cut me off.

"Shh. I don't want to talk about that. Not today."

"It's not my favorite topic either, but we can't just ignore it, right? We both know it's going to happen."

He entangled his fingers in mine. "You're right. We do have to talk about it sooner or later. But today, I want to pretend as if nothing is going to change."

"But things will change."

He threw me a smile. "Oh, Suzie. I haven't felt this high on life in a long time. Why don't we savor it while we can? Have ourselves a magical Christmas and forget we live thousands of miles apart?"

"I don't want this high to end either," I admitted. It was the best feeling in the world. Being with Alex made me feel as if I could tackle anything.

He took a paper napkin from the holder and slowly ripped it into small pieces as he spoke.

"You know, you could stay here. Take over the store for real, not just temporarily. That is, if your boss agrees. You could start a life here. I'm not asking you to marry me or anything, but we could try to make this work."

I bit my lip. How could I give up everything I had back in Los Angeles? My job, my friends, my comfort zone. My heart screamed that I wanted nothing more than to be close to Alex, but I had to be responsible. I couldn't leave my life behind and start somewhere fresh just because of a couple of kisses.

"I know it sounds crazy, and that you've got a life in California."

"I honestly don't know what to say to that," I said. "It does sound tempting though."

"You don't have to say anything. At least not for now."

Leanne put two bags on our table. "Two grilled cheese sandwiches. Enjoy," she said. She even threw me a smile.

"Will you walk me to my car?" I asked Alex.

"It would be my pleasure."

We settled our bills and then went out and crossed the street, stopping at my rental car.

Alex leaned in and kissed me, slowly, like he wanted to taste every inch of me, and I let him. How would I ever be able to turn my back on this blooming connection between us?

"We'll make this work. Somehow. We'll find a way. I promise," I whispered and got into my car.

As I drove off, I could see Alex in the rearview mirror, getting smaller with every passing second until he was completely out of sight. A gut-wrenching feeling settled inside of me. Was this how I was going to feel next week when we would inevitably have to say goodbye to each other?

I was looking forward to returning to my familiar life, yet deep down I hoped Kate's applicant turned out to be a bad fit and that she would ask me to stay in Old Pine Cove much, much longer.

CHAPTER SEVENTEEN

I didn't have any time to think about a possible future with Alex for the rest of the afternoon. In fact, I didn't have a spare minute to think about anything but work. The reading and signing had drawn hundreds of people to Got It Covered, which was a lot more than I'd expected. I was lucky to have Addy there to help me. She handed out hot cocoa to the people waiting outside until they could squeeze themselves through the door and get in line to get their hands on Becca's new book. Thank goodness I had plenty of copies in the stock room, since the person trashing the bookstore had ruined so many copies.

I manned the register and rang up book after book, while Becca smiled and talked with every single customer and posed for pictures. We worked together like a well-oiled machine.

At half past three, Hugo made his way through the crowd, something I had to applaud him for. Everyone thought he wanted to cut in line, but he'd been smart enough to hold his press credentials in the air so his pathway to the door was wide open.

"This is the busiest I've ever seen a store in this town," he told me, his eyes sparkling with delight. "Do you mind if I interview a couple of people for the local paper and the website?"

"Of course not. I'm sure almost everyone here is more than willing to answer any questions you have about the event. If you hang around for a while, you might even get the chance to have a short conversation with Becca Loveheart."

"Thank you, Suzie. I'll be sad to see you go when your colleague takes over. Diane told me they've found someone."

I frowned. "She did? Well, I'm afraid that information isn't one hundred percent correct. They are working on it, but nothing is set in stone yet." *And it's none of Diane's business either what happens to the store.*

Hugo let out a laugh. "You know what they say, always double-check your sources or you'll look like a fool. We both know Diane's information can often be taken with a grain of salt," he added with a wink, then set out to find a couple of people to interview.

Now Diane was spreading so-called facts about the new store manager? It was like that old witch took pleasure in the fact that I would be leaving soon, the way she loved to rub my nose in it. What had I ever done to spite her apart from ruining Christmas a decade ago? It was ridiculous that a septuagenarian with red nail polish and ridiculously perfect coiffed hair could make my blood boil like that, but I couldn't help myself. If only I could tell her I'd be just as happy to not ever have to see her again either.

"They're here," Addy called out to me, rushing inside.

I tried to see who she was referring to, but all I could see was a delivery guy struggling to get through the customers lining up.

"I'm sorry, who are you talking about?"

"The calendars of course!"

With all the kissing that had been going on, I had totally forgotten that the calendars would arrive today.

"Do you want to do the honors?" Addy asked while putting one of the boxes on the counter.

"I totally do." I took a pair of scissors and let it slide through the packing tape. Excitement rushed through me as I opened the box to reveal the calendar. There it was, in all its glory.

I took a copy and leafed through it. Alex and I looked like a Hollywood couple, all sparkling and smiling.

"Are those for sale? Because if they are, I want one," said a forty-something woman who was waiting for her book to be rung up.

"Me too. And one for my sister," another lady exclaimed.

People started to swarm together to take a look at the goods. Alex's goods. For sure someone had tinkered with the images. It was like Alex's features got accentuated to make him look even more irresistible.

"Isn't that you in those pictures? You are one lucky woman," someone said.

"I need that stud in my office. You know what? Make it five, so I can give a copy to all of my colleagues at the beauty salon," a woman in a red coat said, almost snagging the calendar out of my hands.

"These calendars are for sale, yes, and the proceeds will go to a good cause," I said.

They were supposed to be sold during the Winter Walk, but I had buyers right in front of me and I should take advantage of the opportunity. It wasn't like anyone cared who bought them, as long as I could donate a big chunk to charity.

The calendars sold like hotcakes and by the time the last person closed the door of the store behind her, I couldn't feel my feet anymore.

"This was such a fun event," Becca said, stretching her arms and flexing her legs. "And I'm sure you don't mind if I take one of these home with me, do you?" She took a calendar out of the almost-empty box and tucked it away in her bag without waiting for my reply.

"I'm happy that this was such a positive experience for you," I said. "Thank you so much for agreeing to do a signing at a small bookstore like this one. I know you normally go for the bigger venues."

"Oh, that's my publisher who wants me to go to those places. Not that I mind of course, but I actually love more intimate settings like this. I should see if I can convince them to do this kind of thing more often."

"Will you stay for the Winter Walk?" I asked. "I can add you to the list, even though the event is technically sold out."

"I don't see why not. I don't leave until tomorrow morning and Addy hasn't stopped talking about this event ever since I arrived at the inn."

"One of the starting points is Dave's Diner. Shall I walk there with you?"

Becca waved her hand, dismissing my offer, and put her coat on. "I'm fine. I don't mind being alone for a while after the busy afternoon we've had. You girls make sure everything goes smoothly and I'll see you later."

I turned to Addy. "Let's start by putting the cakes on the table over there, and then we can put blankets on the chairs for that extra cozy vibe."

We only had about an hour and a half hour before people would start arriving. Alex had been nice enough to rearrange the layout of the store so that we would have maximum capacity. The Christmas lights were shining brightly and I had added fake snow around the big armchair I was going to use to read the Christmas story we had picked out for our stop of the Winter Walk.

"A little birdie told me you and Alex looked pretty cozy today," Addy said, placing a cinnamon cake on one of the tables.

"How on earth is that possible? Who told you?"

Addy let out a giggle. "Nothing happens in a small town

like this without everyone knowing about it. At least not when something happens in public. You should've figured that one out by now."

I grinned. "What do you think happened?"

"You two ordered lunch together, looking all loved up. Why, did something else happen?"

"If I tell you something, do you promise not to tell anyone?"

She pretended to lock her lips and looked at me expectantly.

"Alex and I kissed."

"What? When? How?" she squealed.

I put down the stack of plates I was holding and leaned against the table. "Last night, after we discovered the store had been damaged, I went over there to ask him if he had any spare Christmas decorations I could use. And, well, one thing led to another," I said. I couldn't get the ridiculous smile off my face, and I was sure I looked like an infatuated teenager. "And we may also have kissed today, by my car."

"I knew there was something more going on between you two."

"He even asked me to stay."

Addy's eyes widened. "He asked you to stay?" she screamed.

"Shhh. Not so loud. I don't want the entire neighborhood to know," I said, even though there wasn't a single soul around.

"Well, are you? Staying?" she asked, keeping her voice

down this time.

"I don't know how that would work. Yes, I have feelings for Alex, big feelings even. But I don't know if leaving everything behind for him would be a good idea. I'm also not sure if that's what I want."

"If you want my advice, follow your heart. There's nothing worse than letting the one you love slip through your fingers. It's scary, yes, but never knowing what could've been is even worse than that."

"Don't you think love is too strong a word? I like him a lot, but let's be honest, I barely know him."

Addy placed a hand on my arm. "Suzie, you *know* Alex. You might not have spent a lot of time together yet, but from what I hear, your connection runs deep. Sometimes it doesn't take a whole lot of time to figure out who your heart belongs to."

"I did promise him we would find a way to make it work," I said, Addy's words resonating with me.

"See? That's your heart talking right there." She smiled and went to the kitchen to retrieve the last couple of cakes that needed to be cut for the event. I looked outside and saw Alex approaching the store. When he caught my eye, a big smile lit up his beautiful face and reached all the way to his eyes. My heart had already given itself to Alex, and my head better get used to it.

CHAPTER EIGHTEEN

Alex walked in looking as if he was going to a fancy party instead of a walk through his hometown. I had to restrain myself from kissing him then and there.

"You look amazing," I said.

"I have something special planned for tonight, and a special occasion calls for a special outfit, doesn't it?"

"Hey, Alex," Addy said, walking back in with the last cake.

"I'm about to start my round of all the stops in town and I thought I'd start here," he said. "If there's any last-minute problem or question concerning the Winter Walk, now would be the perfect time to let me know."

I looked around the store at the yellow armchair decked

out with a sheepskin blanket, the folded chairs with blankets on them and the Christmas tree shining in all its glory. "We're all set here. No problems or questions."

"We do have something fun for you," Addy said. She walked over to the counter and took one of the calendars from the stack.

Alex whistled. "This looks great. And in such a short time. I've got to say I'm impressed."

"You two look perfect together," Addy said.

"We already sold about a hundred copies." I tried to steer the conversation away from Alex and me being a perfect couple. It was not something I wanted to discuss with an audience around.

"The ladies at the signing liked what they saw." Addy winked at Alex, who laughed at the comment.

"I don't know whether to be creeped out or flattered by that," Alex said, tucking the calendar under his arm. "Anyway, I'd better head out and check on the other shops participating in the Winter Walk, but I'll be back around nine to pick you up."

"Me?" I asked.

"Yes, you. Wear warm clothes. That's all I'm telling you," he said. Then he turned around and exited the store, leaving me wondering where he was going to take me.

***

Right on the dot, people started trickling in. I read a Christmas story every fifteen minutes, and after each one,

Addy and I served hot chocolate, mulled wine and slices of cake to the participants. Time flew by and before we knew it, it was almost time to close up again.

"I'm so happy to see this store back in business," an old lady with greyish hair said to me after the last reading. She had her hands around a cup of mulled wine and looked around with a contented smile. "Right there in the corner, where the notebooks are, that's where we would meet for our weekly book club," she said, pointing her long finger.

"Really? I didn't know that," I replied.

She nodded. "Oh, yes, there's so much history in this place. There used to be comfy armchairs and a small table where we all gathered our treats. Cookies, cinnamon rolls... Irene even made a layered cake once for Christmas, little marzipan Santas on top and everything."

I finished pouring a cup of hot cocoa and put the can down. "That sounds like a lot of fun. What kind of books did your book club read?"

"Romances mostly, although we did enjoy the odd thriller. Mind you, we spent most of the time talking about things other than books. It was nice to get out of the house and chat with like-minded people. We sure had a lot of laughs." A sad look crossed her face for just one second.

"I never thought about having a book club in here. You make it sound absolutely adorable."

She smiled. "It was. But I won't keep you occupied any longer with my nostalgic stories."

"Oh, come on, I love to hear about the history of the store," I protested.

"There are lots of stories I can share with you, but on another day. Trust me, when a handsome man is waiting for you, you don't want to keep talking to an old lady like me."

"What are you talking about?"

I turned around and spotted Alex leaning near the counter. I smiled at him and he walked toward us. "I see you've met Sarah," he said.

"We were just talking about the book club that used to meet in here. Isn't that fantastic? I think we should bring that old tradition back to life," I said. Then I realized I wouldn't be around for that.

Alex smiled. "I'm sorry to interrupt you two, but I'm going to kidnap Suzie here for the rest of the night."

"I'll lock everything up," said Addy, who was now standing right next to me. "As long as you promise to follow your heart," she added in a whisper.

Alex and I said goodbye to everyone and stepped outside. The entire neighborhood looked like a magical winter wonderland.

Alex led me to his car and opened the door for me. He held my hand so I wouldn't slip while getting in before walking around the car and getting into the driver's seat.

He leaned in and pressed his lips gently to mine, one hand holding the back of my head, the other resting softly on my arm. His kiss stirred the butterflies in my stomach.

"I've wanted to do that again ever since lunch," he said.

"I'm glad you did," I grinned.

He adjusted the rearview mirror and started the engine.

"Let's get going, shall we?"

We rolled up the mountain in silence and I marveled at the thousands of lights flickering in the village below.

Alex parked the car at the ski resort and led me up a small path. It was so small that I would've missed it if he hadn't pointed it out to me.

"I hope this isn't the part in our story where you turn out to be a serial killer," I said. The trees stood looming in the dark and a chill went through me, not from the cold this time.

He squeezed my hand. "Do you trust me?" He gave me a sideways glance.

"I trust you."

Right around the first bend, some lights came into view and the atmosphere quickly turned from creepy to romantic. The entire path was flanked by big glass containers filled with candles, their flames dancing in the moonlight. The path kept winding up until we arrived at a big clearing. Wooden banisters marked the edge of the clearing and in the middle there was a big table, complete with a red tablecloth and matching napkins.

"Is this for us?" I asked, stating the obvious.

"When you said you'd never been swept off your feet by a romantic gesture I felt that I should at least try to give you a night to remember. Whether you stick around Old Pine Cove or not."

He trailed a finger over my cheek, all the way down to my shoulder and elbow, before entwining his fingers with mine.

I planted a kiss on his warm mouth. "Thank you." It came out as an almost inaudible whisper, but inside I was screaming with gratitude and joy.

He pulled out one of the chairs and I sat down. I'd never seen so many stars, apart from that time Dean and I spent the night at the Grand Canyon camping site. And when I say night, I mean one hour and twenty minutes. Dean was too freaked out by the possibility of finding a bug in his sleeping bag that he refused to spend an entire night there.

"How did you find this spot?" I asked.

"I used to come here with my friends when I was younger – before the resort bought all the surrounding land, that is. Let's say I know someone in high places who pulled some strings for us."

"I should broaden my social circle then, if these are the benefits of that," I joked.

As if materializing out of thin air, a waiter came out with two steaming plates of spaghetti and a bottle of red wine. He put everything on the table before discreetly disappearing again.

"You remembered," I said, gesturing at my favorite dish. "And you even let them bring extra cheese."

"I remember more than you think." Alex reached over and briefly touched my hand. "Your favorite dish, the way you drink your coffee, how you can't stand it when people try to cut in line just because they don't have a full shopping cart. And your love for kissing books, which is adorable. I don't like kissing books myself, but I do like kissing you."

"We clearly have a lot in common."

He put his fork down and pinned me in place with a look that screamed desire. "You also made me remember what it's like to love someone so much that it hurts, physically hurts, to think about them leaving. I didn't think I'd ever be able to feel something like that again after Heather left me."

I shoved a bite of spaghetti into my mouth to give myself some extra moments before answering. Alex threw me a smile so sweet that I had to restrain myself from lurching forward and kissing him, long and hard. I dabbed my mouth with my napkin and folded my hands.

"At first, I didn't want to come here. I begged my boss to please send me somewhere else, but she wouldn't have it. I thought this trip was going to be boring, but most of all, I was scared. Scared you'd still live here and that I would remember how much fun we had all those years ago. Scared of losing myself, of not being able to stop myself from falling. For you."

"And how did that turn out?"

I smiled. "It's like I have a sixth sense, because I *haven't* been able to stop myself from falling for you. I don't know how to deal with that. I don't like change, and this will change everything for me."

My heart raced like a horse on steroids. I half expected Alex to start laughing and tell me that this had all been an elaborate joke, but all he did was stand up and take my hand.

He led me to the edge of the raised platform. He stood

behind me and enveloped me in a hug, warming my back. I could feel his breath on my neck as he whispered into my ear. "If you don't stay, then I will follow you. They offer chef studies in Los Angeles as well. I'm not letting you go twice in one lifetime."

I turned around and searched his eyes for a trace of doubt. "I can't ask you to uproot your life like that. You've got a life here."

He planted soft kisses on my face. "I do. But what is life without the person you care about? What use is it if you never shake things up and do what truly makes you happy? I don't want to die full of regrets one day. I want to be able to say I did everything I in my power to be the happiest I could be. That includes making this work. You and me."

"Kind of like better to try and fail than never try at all?"

He laughed. "Something like that. Although I prefer to try and succeed massively."

I couldn't care less that my spaghetti was getting cold, or that my toes were starting to freeze, or that I had an itch on my leg that was screaming to be scratched. All I cared about was being close to Alex and filling myself up with his warmth.

"Close your eyes for a moment."

He put a small box in my hand and wrapped my fingers around it.

"Now you can open them. And this."

I removed the red wrapping paper and golden bow and opened the box. I pulled out the gift and gasped. Inside was a snow globe with a miniature bookstore. I shook it.

Thick snowflakes fell onto the roof of the shop.

"This is just perfect. Thank you." I smiled as I trailed my hand over the gift. To think that I'd gotten him a snow globe as well. We were so in tune with each other.

"Now you'll always have something to remember these last few weeks by."

"I do," I said. "But I'll also have you."

I grabbed the collar of his coat and pulled him closer, until our faces were only inches apart. Then I kissed him, until the world around us faded and there was only me, him and the explosion of unspoken feelings between us.

CHAPTER NINETEEN

The next morning I woke up around seven a.m. and immediately grabbed my phone from the nightstand. I sent a quick text to Alex, telling him how I couldn't wait to have lunch together. Mere seconds later, my phone rang. He was clearly missing me.

"I'm afraid I'm going to have to cancel our plans today," he said. "I woke up not feeling too well."

I felt my stomach drop at the thought of not seeing him any time soon, but his health was more important. He must've caught something up on that mountain the night before.

"Is there anything I can do? Should I come by and make you some soup?" I offered.

"No, please don't drop by. I wouldn't want you to get

sick too. I'm going to crawl back into bed and I'm sure I'll feel better soon."

"What about the Snow Ball? Will you make it?"

There was a beat of silence before he replied. "Maybe. I'll let you know, is that okay?"

"Okay. But you do know you can call me if you need anything, right? No matter the hour."

"Thank you, Suzie," he said. He hesitated for a moment. "I'm sorry to do this to you. I hadn't planned it. We'll talk later. I promise."

I let out a small laugh. "Nobody ever plans on getting sick. Don't worry about it. All you have to focus on is getting better."

We exchanged our goodbyes, but I couldn't shake the feeling that something wasn't right. Alex had seemed perfectly fine when I'd last seen him a mere ten hours before, and he sure didn't mention feeling unwell then.

I sighed and tried to push away these ridiculous thoughts. There was no rhyme or reason when it came to illness. Like I'd told Alex myself, nobody planned on getting sick.

I threw the duvet aside and stepped into the shower. Alex and I had decided to make this work. He would visit me in California next month for a couple of weeks and then we'd decide on a further plan of action. I smiled at the thought of him meeting my friends and seeing where I lived. We could go for walks on the beach every night or stay in and order takeout. It was going to be amazing.

After my shower, I brought my inner Martha Stewart to the surface and made a batch of apple cupcakes, from scratch. That was bound to make him feel better.

I stacked the cupcakes in a container and put them in a bag together with a fresh fruit salad. Stepping outside, I could see that the weather was taking a turn for the worse. Dark gray clouds hung low and a chilly wind had gathered force.

The curtains of Alex's house were still drawn, even though it was way past eleven. Poor Alex. He was probably so sick that he hadn't even made it out of bed.

A white Audi was parked in the driveway, with a vanity plate reading QN HTHR. I wondered who it belonged to. Maybe he had called a nurse? Or his sister had come to visit?

I walked up the steps to the front door, careful not to slip, and rang the doorbell.

The door swung open and a woman I didn't recognize stood in front of me. Her blonde hair spilled over her shoulders and she threw me an annoyed look.

"Yes?" she asked with a hand on her hip.

"Is Alex around?" I took a step forward, ready to step inside, but she extended her arm so that the doorway was blocked.

"Who wants to know?"

"I'm Suzie, I live next door. Are you Alex's nurse?"

She laughed so hard that tears sprang to her eyes. "His nurse? That is golden."

I arched an eyebrow. What was so weird about that question?

"If you must know, I'm Heather. Alex's fiancée," she

added with a look of pride.

Now it was my turn to laugh. "Yeah, I'm sorry, I thought you said you're Alex's fiancée, but that's not possible. She left without a trace a year ago."

"And now she's back," she said.

Alex had lied to me? I suddenly felt nauseous, but reprimanded myself. There was no use jumping to conclusions. I was sure there had to be a logical explanation for all of this.

"I need to see Alex," I said and stepped forward. Heather grabbed my arm and stopped me in my tracks.

"Look, Suzie, right?"

I nodded.

"I'm sorry to break it to you, but whatever you thought you and Alex had, it's over."

I shook my head in disbelief.

"Alex told me that there's nothing going on between you," she said. "Nothing more than some fling. You're leaving soon, aren't you? He thought he had feelings for you, until I showed up again and he remembered how much he loved me. We share a past together. I'm sorry to have to say this to you, but it's all true."

My mouth tried to form words, but my vocal chords didn't cooperate.

"Oh, and I'm taking over the bookstore next door, so there's no need for you to stick around any longer," she added.

"You what?" I asked, but she slammed the door in my face without answering. I turned around and tried to run, but it felt as if something was literally holding me back.

I looked over my shoulder and saw that a piece of my coat was stuck in the door. Great. I tried to yank it loose, tears streaming over my cheeks, but the fabric wouldn't budge.

I pounded on the door and Heather appeared again. "Can I help you with something?"

"You've done enough," I said with a squeaking voice and ran down the stairs. Back at the bookstore, I locked the door and made my way up to the bedroom. I was shaking as I crawled under the covers, a dark stone settling itself in the pit of my stomach. Heather was taking everything I loved away from me. Alex. The bookstore I'd worked so hard to make a success. My belief that true love and second chances were possible for me.

After half an hour, a clear thought made its way through the mist of my sorrow. Maybe Heather wasn't telling the truth. Maybe she just wanted to get rid of me and have Alex all to herself. I wiped away the snot and tears and dialed Alex's number. If I could talk to him, this whole nightmare would be over soon.

But the phone kept ringing, no matter how many times I tried to get through to him. After twelve attempts, I stopped trying and sent him a text instead, asking him to please call me.

Everything went silent for at least an hour and a dark cloud settled in my heart. How stupid had I been to think I could get my fairytale here? I'd known Alex for a few weeks. He and Heather had known each other way longer.

The sound of the doorbell made me rush downstairs, hope building once again. But instead of Alex, it was Addy. Sweet Addy, who had been nothing but nice to me ever since I'd arrived in Old Pine Cove.

"What's wrong?" she asked, putting an arm around my shoulder. "Why are you crying?"

"Heather is over at Alex's. She told me Alex doesn't want to see me anymore," I said, the words coming out in choked little tidbits.

Her eyes grew wide with surprise. "What are you talking about? Heather is here? *The* Heather?"

I pointed at Heather's car to make my point. "See?" I wanted to take my house keys and scratch her car front to back. Or stab them in her stomach and turn them around.

Addy frowned. "That's... weird. There must be a logical explanation for this."

"Is there? Alex is not even answering my calls."

"That doesn't sound like Alex at all. Why don't I go over there to figure out what's going on?"

I grabbed her by the arm and pulled her inside. "No, no, no. Please don't go over there."

"Why not? Are you afraid I'll catch them... you know? Because I highly doubt that. Heather broke Alex's heart, big time. There's no way he's letting her back into his life."

Alex and Heather going at it hadn't crossed my mind before, but now I couldn't get the image out of my head. They'd be having sex, no question about it. The kind two people have when they realize they belong together.

I stumped up the stairs, followed by Addy, and took my

suitcase from under the bed.

Addy's eyes grew wide. "You're leaving?"

"There's nothing here for me anymore. Not the store. Not Alex. Nada."

She looked at me as if I'd stabbed her with a knife, a mix of disbelief and hurt all mingled into one.

"I'm sorry, Addy. I didn't mean that you don't matter," I said, throwing clothes into my suitcase without bothering to fold them first. "I need to get away. But I promise you that we'll stay friends no matter what, okay?"

"Where will you go? It's Christmas Eve, Suzie," she said with a soft voice.

"Home." I ran around the house, throwing all of my belongings into my suitcases while Addy was listing off reasons on her fingers for me to stay.

"Please, Suze, don't leave like a thief in the night," she pleaded. "I'm sure all of this can still be salvaged. I'm sure it's nothing more than a stupid misunderstanding."

"I won't be able to breathe with *them* next door," I said and made my way downstairs. I took one last look at Got It Covered. I had loved the place, but now it was tainted. Like a yummy drink with a bad aftertaste. Addy squeezed my arm without saying a word. It was clear that there was no stopping me.

"Be safe, okay?" she said, helping me heave my luggage into my rental car.

I closed the trunk and pulled her in for a hug. "Thank you for wanting me to stay. Oh, and will you throw this away for me?" I handed her a gift box. There was no way

I'd be able to give Alex his snow globe now.

"What is it?"

"It was going to be a gift. I'd rather smash it against Alex's house, but that would be a waste. If you don't want to throw it away, you can keep it at the inn."

"Oh, Suzie." A sad look crossed her face.

"Thanks again. For everything."

I started the engine and pulled away. Away from the bookstore, from Old Pine Cove, from Alex. I drove until the entire town disappeared, as if I'd never been there at all.

The tears came down again, big and full of understanding that nothing would ever be the same again.

***

"What do you mean all flights to L.A. are full?"

"I'm sorry, miss, but it's Christmas Eve. Any other day you'd be able to fly out, but not today. Is there any other way I can help you?"

"I wish there was. Could you perhaps fix everything that's wrong with my life, Patricia?" I asked, glancing at her nametag.

Her eyes grew as wide as saucers. "Are you going to yell at me if I say no?"

"Of course not," I said in a brittle voice. "I'm sorry, I'm just having a bad day."

She gave me a short nod. "If you want to fly out to

somewhere else, let me know, okay?"

"Thanks."

I walked away from the ticket desk and sat down in one of the nearby plastic chairs. I swallowed hard. There was no way I'd sob at an airport on one of the busiest days of the year.

I pulled my phone out of my bag. There were two missed calls from Alex and a text that said *call me*.

With trembling fingers, I called him back. Maybe he had a good explanation for all of this. Maybe Heather had been lying to me. I owed him a chance to explain. He picked up at the first ring.

"Suzie, where are you?"

Hearing his voice made it difficult to push back the tears. "I'm at the airport. Is it true? Is Heather taking over the bookstore?"

A beat of silence confirmed that she had told me the truth after all. Gosh, I'd been so stupid.

I took a deep breath in. "Is she still there with you? In your house?"

"She is. But it's not what you think," Alex said. "Don't run away like this without knowing exactly what happened between Heather and me."

"I know enough," I said, and shut off my phone.

I looked around the airport, wanting to get out of here as soon as possible. I felt trapped. I couldn't go back to Old Pine Cove. How embarrassing would that be? To make a run for it only to return half a day later, because all flights home were full. I should've known that ideal runaway scenarios only happen in movies, not in real life.

I considered flying out to my sister's to be with my family, but that wasn't a good idea either. My sister was about to have a baby. I didn't want to bum them out with my sobfest.

I aimlessly scrolled through my phone, as if the answers were hidden inside the small device somewhere, and then it hit me. I knew exactly where to go.

CHAPTER TWENTY

I pushed through the crowd of people, eager to get away from the airport and drink eggnog on the beach, when I saw an enormous cardboard sign that said *Welcome to the madness, Suzie.*

I laughed and snatched the cardboard out of its owner's hands. "The madder, the better," I said and pulled Dean into a hug. "I can't tell you how happy I am to see you."

"Are you sure you're up for this kind of crazy?" Dean asked, the two of us still hugging. "I swear it's a whole different level of madness."

I grinned. "You better believe I am."

As we left Miami Airport, I was able to relax a little. The sun was shining bright and there was not a patch of snow in sight, apart from the fake kind. It was hard to believe that I had woken up in a snowy small town, and now I was cruising along the highway to spend Christmas at a beach in Florida.

"You think I'm crazy for running off to someone else's Christmas party, don't you?" I asked, putting my feet up on the dashboard.

"I already knew you were crazy, honey," Dean said. "That's why I got you something."

As soon as the traffic lights turned to red, he bent down and pulled a bag from under his seat.

"You're quite the magician," I said and took the package from him. Inside were a couple of shirts that said *I love Miami*, a pair of tacky flip-flops with hotdogs on them and a blue summer dress.

"I figured you'd have nothing to wear except for winter gear," he said.

"Thank you. I hadn't even thought about the logistics of this," I said and swapped my boots for the hotdog flip-flops. I rolled down the window, flexed my toes and closed my eyes.

"Much better," I mumbled.

Dean threw me a sideways glance. "So… he broke your heart, huh?"

I winced. "It still doesn't make any sense to me. One moment he was being all romantic and telling me he saw a future with me, and the next he's shacking up with his ex again after she broke his heart. I don't think I'll ever understand men."

Dean laughed. "So one guy screws you over and suddenly it's the entire male race's fault?"

I poked his arm with my finger. "As if men never say something like that about women."

"There's one thing I don't understand though," he said. "I told you earlier this month how boring and crazy my family is and yet you decided to join me and spend Christmas with them?"

I shrugged. "They can't be that bad, Dean. I mean, come on."

A mischievous grin traveled all the way up to his eyes. "Don't say I didn't warn you."

One hour later, we pulled into the driveway of a beach house. I'm sorry, beach *mansion*. The driveway was filled with expensive cars. As I peeked inside, I marveled at the leather interiors and big dashboard consoles they boasted.

"Your family is rich," I said, stating the obvious.

Dean scrunched his nose. "And rich in judgements."

"If they serve gold bars for dinner, they can judge me all they want," I said with a laugh.

The front door was so tall that a family of giants could pass through. I was about to use the obnoxiously big lion-shaped copper knocker when Dean put a hand on my arm.

"That thing's only there for decoration purposes."

He put his key in the lock, and we walked in.

"You've brought a girl," I heard a woman say. "You've brought a girl home for Christmas!"

A woman in navy slacks and a white blouse joined us in the hallway. She was wearing a pearl necklace and matching pearl earrings. Her hair was tied back so tight that it pulled on the skin of her face. Or maybe she'd had a facelift?

"Suzie, this is Jane, my mother."

Jane didn't reply, but instead called out into the empty space. "Charles! You have to get down here now. Dean brought a girl home for Christmas."

Dean and I exchanged a look and he rolled his eyes at his mother. "You do realize I'm still gay, right? This doesn't change anything," he said, motioning at me with his hands.

"We'll see. We'll see," she said. "Let's get you two some drinks."

***

Three hours, fifteen appetizers, and a handful of cocktails later, I was afraid to stand up. Even sitting down, the world seemed to be turning too fast for my fancy.

I wasn't fond of getting drunk, but Dean had been right all along. His family brought crazy to a whole new level. As in, they were crazy good at judging people. They also tried to impress each other with terminology no one understood and boasted about achievements I was sure no one cared about. Dean and I had turned it into a game. We decided we would down a cocktail every time someone came up to us to tell another incredibly boring and arrogant story.

"Do you want to get out of here?" Dean asked now with a slur in his voice.

"Where would we go? We're both a bit unstable at the moment," I answered.

He shoved his chair back. Then he pulled me from mine, making the world swirl in front of me. He pointed to a narrow path at the back of the garden.

"Let's go skinny-dipping. No one will even notice we're gone."

"We should bring towels and food," I said, not even thinking about how ridiculous it was to swim in the ocean naked on Christmas Eve.

"I'll be right back. Don't move," Dean said, and zigzagged his way inside.

I took my phone out to kill the time and saw that I had five missed calls from Addy. I quickly sent her a text. I told her I was going skinny-dipping in Florida, that she didn't have to worry about me and that I'd call her later. At least, that's what I hoped I had written. Autocorrect and cocktails didn't go together that well.

"Ready?" Dean stood in front of me with a bag full of towels and a big box.

"What are you hiding in that box?"

"It's chocolate cake," he said. "I snatched it out of the fridge."

"Marry me."

We walked toward the beach, laughing and stumbling. Then we stripped down to our underwear and jumped into the ocean.

As the cool water hit my skin, I forgot all about my troubles. The alcohol and the nearness of my best friend had thrown me into a different reality, one where there was no Alex and no heartbreak, and I was just Suzie again.

***

I didn't even know how I had gotten into a bed, although I had a vague recollection of Dean and me sneaking into the guest house. I forced myself to open my eyes and surveyed the damage. There were smears of chocolate marking the crumpled sheets on the bed. Dean was sprawled on the floor with nothing but his underwear on, the cake box was open beside him.

I stepped over him and stumbled into the shower, drinking from the water that ran over my body. I'd probably have to drink three bathtubs of water before I'd find myself hydrated again.

I toweled myself dry and got dressed, then kneeled beside Dean. He looked even worse than me.

"Merry Christmas, buddy," I said.

"What time is it?"

"It's almost eleven."

He groaned. "Dammit. We have to be back at the house at eleven for the Christmas brunch. It's tradition."

I looked at the wall clock that was mounted above the bed. "Well, we've still got seven minutes left. No harm, no foul."

Dean dragged himself into the bathroom. I lay down on the bed, my thoughts circling back to Alex. I didn't know how to feel about him. Should I hate him for what he'd done to me? I wanted to, so badly, but when I thought about him smiling at me, I couldn't help but feel my heart melt.

"You know you don't have to join me for brunch, right?" Dean said, coming back in with a towel around his waist.

"I know, I don't mind," I said. "But no drinking this time."

Dean made a gagging sound. "Hell, no. I'm never drinking again."

"Me neither."

With one minute left to spare, we rushed out of the beach house and to the main house. Jane was waiting for us at the back door, wringing her hands. "There you two are," she said with an anxious smile.

I threw her a sheepish look as if we were two naughty teenagers who'd run off to some party the night before.

"There's someone here for you, Suzie." She looked at her golden watch. "He's been waiting for more than two hours already."

"Me?" I asked. "That's impossible. No one knows I'm here."

Jane turned on her heel and we followed her inside. As I rounded the corner and caught a glimpse of the table, my heart stopped in my throat.

Sitting between Dean's teenage cousins was Alex. I blinked. Was I dreaming? Was I still drunk?

He got up and his chair fell to the ground with a loud bang. The room grew quiet and I froze in place.

"What... how... you..."

"Suzie," Alex began. "Maybe we can go outside and talk?"

What was he doing here? How did he get here? The questions kept bumping against each other, each one fighting for a chance to be uttered first.

Without talking, I walked outside again. Dean's family kept quiet, following our every move. Who would've guessed that this was the way to make them shut up for a while?

Alex followed me into the garden and grabbed my hand.

"What are you doing here, Alex?" I asked. "Is Heather going to jump out of the bushes as well?"

He looked me straight in the eye. "Heather and I are history."

"Yeah," I said with a huff. "That's what you told me before and yet that turned out to be a lie. You're a liar. And a... a... You're..."

"In love with you," he said.

"You are?"

He cupped my face in his hands. "I am."

"Then why did Heather tell me you guys were back together?" I asked, pushing his hands away, but he immediately put them right back. "You told me she was at your house when we were on the phone yesterday. Was that a lie as well?"

"She showed up out of the blue, claiming that we needed to make it work again, that she'd been wrong for turning me down. But I told her my heart was taken. By you."

"But then why didn't you answer the door when I dropped by?"

A pained expression crossed over his face. "I was in

the shower. When I realized what had happened, you were gone already. Addy told me you left in a hurry after talking with Heather and I didn't know what to do. I needed time to think, to process everything. I wanted to find a way to tell you about Heather taking over the store without it sounding like I knew about it. I swear I didn't."

I looked up at him. There was nothing but honesty in his eyes. "And you feeling sick? You sure don't look sick to me."

Alex shook his head. "It wasn't a lie. Heather showing up made me physically ill. But as soon as I knew the truth, my feelings of nausea got replaced by relief. Then fear of having you slip through my fingers."

My heart skipped a beat.

"How did she even know about the job opening?" I asked.

"Heather's sister works at the hospital Diane stayed at when she broke her hip. You know how talkative she is. I'm so sorry, Suzie."

"One simple phone call. That's all it would've taken for you to tell me the truth. Heck, you called me when I was at the airport and all you said was that things were not what I thought they were. Could you have been any vaguer?"

He turned his gaze down. "I was confused. I didn't know what to do and you ran away. You know running away is never the solution, Suzie."

I dropped my shoulders down. "I know that now."

"When Addy gave me the gift you'd bought me, I knew that I couldn't let you go without a fight," Alex said.

"My gift? The snow globe?"

"Yes. But by then, it was already too late. You were gone and I had to stay in Old Pine Cove for the Snow Ball. That's where I found out Heather was the one who destroyed the store."

I gasped. "What?"

He nodded. "I know, what a shitty thing to do, right? Diane confronted her in front of the entire town. She saw that Heather was wearing a feather earring which looked a lot like the one you found in the store. I hadn't paid any attention to it, as she always wears three different earrings."

"But Diane never set foot in the store. How could she know about the earring?" I asked.

"There was an article about the incident in the special edition of *Old Pine Cove Weekly*. Hugo had included a picture of the "crime scene evidence" as he called it."

"Right, Doug told me he was going to ask Hugo to do that." I shook my head. "I can't believe what a horrible person Heather is. Where is she now? What do we do?"

"Doug told me you could press charges, or, well, your boss could. And if you tell Kate about what happened, I don't think they'll want to hire Heather anymore."

"There's one thing I don't understand, though. Why would she trash the store she was about to become the manager of?"

"I asked her the same thing," Alex said. "She told me she was so jealous of you having it all, that she wanted to do something to hurt you. Heather always wants what she can't have. I guess she didn't think about the possible consequences, but that's Heather. She thought she could waltz back into my life and continue as if nothing had happened. Suzie, I never thought I'd utter these words, but I'm glad she broke my heart and left me. If she hadn't, I would've missed out on the chance to be with you."

"How did you know I was here?" I asked. "Did you pay a fortune-teller to find out where I was?"

Alex smiled that knee-buckling smile of his. "No. I still had your password from when I saved you in the woods that night and used your account to locate your phone."

"Smart move," I said.

"I know you're angry, and if you want to leave, I can't stop you. But I do think that would be a big mistake."

I stared into his eyes, seeing nothing but honesty in them.

"Do you want to try and make this work?" I asked.

"No. I don't want to try. There's no use in trying. I just want to do it. If that means moving so I can be close to you, then that's what I'm going to do. I'll apply to chef schools in L.A. right this second if you want to be with me. I love you," he whispered, melting my heart.

"You do?" I grinned.

"I do. I love you," he said. "I've loved you since the first time I saw you ten years ago. And I'm never letting you go again. All I need to know is... Do you feel the same?"

A big smile bubbled up inside of me.

"Come on, what do you say, Suzie?"

"Just kiss me already."

And as Alex pulled me closer and kissed me with a determination and hunger I'd never experienced before, I just knew. He was the one. He loved me and I loved him right back.

"Merry Christmas, Alex. I love you," I whispered in between his mind-blowing kisses.

"Merry Christmas, Suzie. Merry, merry Christmas."

"Oh, it sure is," I said with a grin.

I let my hands trail the length of his back and kissed him again. I didn't know what was going to happen next, but one thing was certain. I was never going to let my Christmas miracle go.

EPILOGUE

Sixteen months later

As I opened the door to Alex's house, I couldn't believe I was in Old Pine Cove again. Only this time, I wasn't planning on going anywhere any time soon. This time, it was permanent.

Alex had gotten his chef's degree in L.A. while I gained experience as store manager of our L.A. brand. On the nights that Alex was working in a local restaurant to refine his skills, I stayed home and wrote. There was no use putting my dream of publishing a book on the backburner any longer.

But Old Pine Cove had never left my mind. Life was

simple there, and I craved simple. When I told Kate about my plans to leave L.A. for good, she was nothing but supportive. The Old Pine Cove store had grown and could use a set of extra hands. I would run the store together with Pippa, the current manager, but only three days per week so that I still had time to write books.

Luckily, Heather was history. Her application to become store manager had been thrown out, and there wasn't a single person in Old Pine Cove who had a good word left for her after what she did, forcing her to leave the town for good. Alex had sold the engagement ring I'd found in the bathroom, shouting "good riddance" as he left the jewelry store.

"Where do you want this?" Alex asked now, holding a box of books in his hands.

"Just put them in the living room for now."

"Do you want me to put them in your bookcase?"

"No. I mean, that's sweet, but you don't know the system."

He raised his eyebrow and laughed. "There's a system to putting books in a bookcase?"

I put my hand on my hip. "As a matter of fact, yes. You can color code them or organize them by genre or height. There are numerous systems to choose from."

He shook his head and threw me a smile. "Let's just hope I don't regret asking you to move to Old Pine Cove with me. Thank goodness you'll be next door managing the store during the day so that I won't have to witness too much of your craziness."

I slapped him with one of the throw pillows I had brought back from our L.A. apartment. "Watch it, mister. You're lucky to have me."

He took my hands and locked eyes with me. "You're right. I'm the luckiest man alive."

"You are," I said and kissed his soft lips before letting go of his hands.

"Don't walk away, let's make out on our new couch."

I laughed and put the snow globe he had gifted me sixteen months ago on the mantle above the fireplace, right next to the one I had gifted him.

"I'd love to, but we have a lot of unpacking to do, and I promised Addy I'd grab a coffee with her later. We still have to celebrate my book getting published. Besides, I need to hear all the stories about the new guy in her life. But after I get back, I'm all yours."

"All night?"

I laughed and spun around. "I'm yours for the rest of my life, Alex."

He closed the distance between us and smiled. "Are you?"

I held up my hand, showing him my wedding ring, and nodded. "I promised when you made me Suzie Denverton last Christmas, remember?"

"I do. There's no one I'd rather share my name with than you, Suzie."

"And there's no one whose name I'd rather have than yours," I said.

He kissed me and I almost regretted making plans with

Addy. It was okay though, since I was the luckiest girl in Old Pine Cove. Heck, I was the luckiest girl in the whole wide world. I got to go home to Alex Denverton every night for the rest of my life.

SNEAK PEEK: LOVE TO PROVE YOU WRONG

Do you want to read Addy's story? Check out Love to Prove You Wrong, the second book in the Old Pine Cove series! Here's an unedited sneak peek for you.

CHAPTER ONE

"**T**here's a duck in the lobby. A living, quacking duck!"

Uh-oh. Not this again.

Diane's panicked voice reached the reception area of the Old Pine Cove Inn moments before she came bursting in. I plastered on my biggest smile and waited for the rest of her tirade.

She threw her hands in the air while pinning Carter and me down with an ominous look. "Well, you heard me. Don't just stand there like idiots. Do something."

"There's no need to panic. It's a duck, not a lion," Carter said, not looking up from the list of guest reservations he was checking.

Diane rubbed her temples with her well-manicured fingers. A big sigh escaped her mouth as she shook her head. It reminded me of the kind of sigh my cousin utters when her toddler insists on having his sandwich cut into squares, then refuses to eat it.

"I don't care what it is. Animals don't belong inside an inn. It's unsanitary. If this duck doesn't get removed from the premises soon, I can't have Asher's wedding here. What if everyone contracts some nasty disease? We've got seventy people coming from out of town. Seventy!"

"I promise you it won't happen again. I apologize, and so does Duckota," I said.

I stepped away from the front desk and made my way to the lobby where Duckota was frolicking around like the happy duck she was.

"It has a name?" Diane's raised eyebrow told me how ridiculous she thought it was to name a duck.

"She sure does," I said and threw her a weak smile. What was wrong with naming an animal? Dogs and cats got named by their owners. There was no reason ducks should be left behind.

I crouched down behind one of the lounge chairs to get to Duckota's hiding place. She probably took shelter in the secluded spot after hearing Diane's panicked screams. I couldn't blame Duckota, though. Anyone would be scared of Diane when they heard her threw one of her famous tantrums. In fact, I was scared of her myself from time to time.

After a mere ten seconds of chasing Duckota, I got a hold of her. "There. She won't escape anytime soon, I promise."

Diane gave me a curt nod before returning her attention to Lilian, the wedding planner she had brought along. At least now that Duckota was being removed from the lobby,

Diane wouldn't have anything to complain about anymore.

"Addy dear, just a minor remark."

Okay, maybe there was something else. I should've known.

I turned around to face Diane, the duck getting restless in my hands.

"Yes?"

The old lady pointed to the framed photographs above the fireplace. I had hung them there to give the inn an extra cozy feel. "Those pictures will have to go. No one wants to look at someone else's family photos at a wedding."

"Sure, no problem," I said with a smile, even though I could feel my jaw tightening. I probably shouldn't have let her rearrange the inn's interior, but this wedding was too important to argue over small details.

Right on cue, Duckota started quacking. I rushed her outside to put her back in the fenced area I had built for her in the backyard.

Unfortunately, the commotion had been a bit too much for her. As soon as she was back outside, she pooped in my hands. Great, just what I needed.

I wiped my hands on a patch of grass.

"Now listen to me carefully, Duckota. No more escaping. We don't want to lose our best customer, now do we?" I said while snapping the lock shut.

Gosh, now I was talking to a duck? Maybe I needed to get out more. That was easier said than done, though. Between running the inn and managing employees, there was hardly any time left to go out and mingle. Let alone mingle and find a boyfriend.

I got back inside, making a beeline for the employees' bathroom. After a royal amount of soap and water, I got the duck poop and its accompanying smell off my hands.

When I joined Carter at the reception desk, I threw him a look. "Was it really necessary to tell Diane not to panic? You could've just reassured her that we would take care of the duck."

He shrugged. "It's a duck, Addy. None of the other guests have complained about having Duckota around. In fact, they all love her."

"I'm aware of that, but you know what Diane's like."

"A control freak?"

"Well, yeah. She likes to have it her way. And don't forget that her grandson's wedding is going to bring in a lot of money for the inn. Please stop taunting her like that. Besides, she's right about Duckota. She shouldn't be in here, but I don't know how I can prevent her from escaping all the time."

Carter looked up from his paperwork and grinned. "If she keeps it up, you might have to start charging her."

"That won't be necessary, thank goodness. I have high hopes for buying the patch of land next door. As soon as this wedding is over, I'll have all the funds I need to put my name on the title deed. Duckota will be one happy duck when that happens."

Ever since Dad left the management of the inn in my hands, I had dreamt of adding a petting zoo to the place. It would have alpacas, rabbits, chickens, goats, and ducks.

Maybe even a pig or a pony. I'd already gotten a lot of positive comments from guests when I talked to them about my ideas. All I needed were the funds to buy an extra patch of land. Hosting Asher's wedding here would seal the deal – if we kept his grandmother happy, of course. Diane was known for her strong opinions and high maintenance behavior, but I knew how to handle her.

Four more weeks of catering to her needs and fulfilling her requests. Four more weeks of her getting on my nerves.

"Addy?" Carter asked, pulling me out of my thoughts.

"Yes?"

He shoved a piece of paper toward me. "We received a last-minute reservation request last night. Can I allocate room 3E to this guest or should we keep that open for emergencies?"

I shoved the paper back into his direction without giving it a glance. "Of course you can. What emergency would we keep it for? The Queen of England coming to visit Old Pine Cove?"

Carter shrugged. "Just wanted to double-check. I don't want to make any mistakes."

"I love that you do that, but how long have you been working here now? Five months? I trust you, Carter. You don't have to double-check everything with me."

He nodded, then opened the online reservation manager. "Kermit the Frog is all confirmed."

"Who is what now?" I asked.

Carter pointed to the screen. "Kermit the Frog. Says so

right here."

I raised one of my eyebrows and laughed. "Kermit the Frog is going to stay at the Old Pine Cove Inn?"

"Well, I'm assuming that's not his real name. Maybe it's one of those tactics celebrities use to protect their identity."

"Oh, okay," I said. "As long as he's not a serial killer and he has a valid credit card, I'm fine with whatever name this guest uses. I'm going to catch up on some paperwork. Would you mind running to the kitchen and checking up on Alex? He wanted to go over this week's menu with one of us."

"Sure. Got any pointers?"

"As long as he doesn't want to serve duck, it's all good," I said.

Carter laughed. "Great. Oh, and thanks for trusting me. I appreciate it."

As Carter disappeared into the kitchen, I couldn't help but smile as well. The kid was a blessing to have around. Even though he was only twenty-two and had a knack for taunting Diane, he had a great work ethic and never complained when I asked him to do something. Plus, guests loved him. Hiring him had cut into my budget, but the inn was growing so much that I couldn't keep doing all the work by myself anymore. There was only so much time in a day.

I printed out some paperwork and stapled it together before retreating into my office. It was small but cozy. Right after I became the new manager of the inn, I'd taken down the hideous brown wallpaper and replaced it with two layers of white paint. I'd also opted for one teal-colored wall. A splash of color had never hurt anyone.

There was just enough space to open the door without hitting the desk, and the tiny window gave me a stunning, albeit restricted, view of the mountains. Their tops were completely covered in snow in the winter, but now that spring had sprung, the lower slopes were blooming. I loved it.

I slid into my chair and started working on an occupancy rate report that I could use to check our marketing ROI. A mere ten minutes later, someone rang the bell at the reception desk. If it was about the duck again, I'd scream.

I slid my chair back, but when I got out of my office, there was no one to be seen.

"Hello?" I called out.

"Just a minute."

A man was crouched down on the floor at the reception desk, going through his suitcase.

"Here it is." The crouching male got up and slapped his printed reservation on the counter.

When his eyes met mine, my breath got stuck in my throat. He narrowed his eyes, as if he wanted to zoom in on my face. Then his eyes grew wide, and a puff of air left his mouth.

"Fat… I mean, Addy?" he asked.

Oh. My. Word. Did he almost call me Fat Addy? It had been ten years since I'd heard that disgusting nickname. A nickname *he* had made viral in high school after watching that movie *Pitch Perfect*.

I rolled my eyes at him. "Justin Miller. I'd say it's a pleasure, but it really isn't."

He cocked an eyebrow and paired his gaze with a smirk I wanted to slap off his face. "Is that how you talk to all of your guests?"

"Of course not, only the ones I don't like. You're the first one so far, if you must know."

Then it dawned on me. He was staying here. For real. At my inn. I mean, he had a suitcase with him and a printed reservation. It was obvious what his plans were.

"Well, are you going to check me in or what?"

I crossed my arms over my chest. "We're all out of rooms. I'm sorry. There was a double reservation."

Instead of turning around and leaving, he laughed. "I don't think so. The confirmation for this reservation came through this morning."

I snatched his reservation from the counter. "Kermit the Frog? Really? I see you haven't changed one bit."

"What? I love that guy. And I don't want everyone to know I'm back. At least not yet anyway."

A rush of panic coursed through me. He wasn't going to stick around for long, was he?

"Back? What are you doing here, Justin? I thought you had moved. Forever."

He grinned at me. "Asher's wedding, of course. What person would let his best friend get married without his oldest friend there to witness the entire thing? Maybe get up to some mischief before he ties the knot?"

"The wedding's not until next month," I said.

He nodded. "That's right."

"You're staying here for four weeks?"

"I am," he said, handing me a platinum American Express card.

"Don't you have to work? And can't you stay with family?"

He leaned on the counter. "I'm in between projects. And yes, I could stay with family, but I don't want to." He scrunched his nose as if I had asked him if he wanted a complimentary platter of duck poop delivered to his room.

There was nothing I could do but check him in. If he wanted to stay here, I couldn't exactly refuse to, unless I wanted to get entangled in a nasty lawsuit.

I handed him his credit card back, together with the keys to his room. "Your room is located on the third floor. Enjoy your stay."

"Oh, I sure will," he said with a smile, and walked away.

I rolled my eyes again. He hadn't changed one bit. Sure, he looked even hotter than he had back in high school, but what did looks matter if you were rotten inside?

"Was that Justin Miller or do I need glasses?" Suzie, my best friend, whom I met two years ago, asked. She was standing right next to the front door, a big box of books in her arms.

"Let me help you with those," I said, ignoring her question.

I took the box from her and put it in my office. Suzie ran the local bookstore and provided guests of the inn with books at great prices. The order forms flew out the door every week. The reviews we got on travel websites almost always mentioned the unique service, something I was extremely proud of. Granted, it was Suzie who had come up with the idea of "Books in Bed", but the execution had been a team effort.

"Well?" she asked, leaning on my desk.

I turned around and riffled through a drawer of paperwork. I didn't want Suzie to see my shaking hands while I talked to her.

"How come you know Justin Miller?" I asked. "You only moved back here a couple of months ago, and he was long gone by then. Thank goodness."

Suzie walked over to my side of the desk and shoved her phone under my nose. "Um, hello. Justin Miller, star of the hit series *In Dire Need*, not to mention a ton of successful romcom movies. Who doesn't know the guy?"

I snatched the phone from her hands and peered at the pictures Google had pulled up for her. "Huh."

Unfortunately, she didn't stop questioning me. "Come on, Addy, you have to tell me more than huh."

I let out a sigh as I closed the door of the office. I wanted no one to hear what I was about to tell Suzie.

"Remember how I told you about that guy who used to call me Fat Addy in high school? And then everyone started calling me that? Well, he and Justin Miller are the same guy."

Suzie gasped. "No way."

"Him laughing at my expense every chance he got drove

guys away from me. He was the town stud and everyone looked up to him, even though they didn't always agree with his behavior."

"What is he doing here?" Suzie asked. "And at the inn of all places?"

"He and Asher are best friends. He came back here for the wedding."

"I see," she said, then narrowed her eyes. "And Asher? Do we still like him? Or should we hate him as well?"

I shook my head. "Asher has never been rude to me. He never spurred Justin on either. If anything, he tried to get Justin to tone it down with the nicknaming. Not that it helped."

Suzie smiled at me. "Let's just hope he stays out of your hair and that he won't cause any trouble."

I laughed. "Justin Miller *is* trouble, believe me."

Three taps on the door cut our conversation short. I knew it was Carter, as I'd been the one to suggest he use a special knock so that I would immediately know it was him and not some random guest.

"Well, duty calls. But I'll see you tomorrow for the Spring Picnic meeting, right?" I asked.

Suzie nodded. "Alex and I will be there. I told him he'd have to go home alone, though. We're still on for that girls' night out we talked about, right?"

"Definitely."

"Great, I'll see you tomorrow," Suzie said.

She waved me goodbye, and I joined Carter at the reception desk where a demanding guest had almost brought the guy to tears. After resolving the issue and finishing the occupancy report, I closed the reception desk for the night and headed home. It was a good thing I hadn't run into Justin again. How I was going to cope with him around for an entire month, I had no clue, but I did know I had to find a way to stay as far away from him as possible.

As soon as I closed the door of my house behind me, I went into my bedroom and changed into loungewear. My place was located right beside the inn so I could be there in a matter of minutes, if I needed to. It was still secluded enough that I could shut out the world as well. If I didn't, then I'd be catering to guests well into the night. There was always something or someone needing my attention, but I was only human after all.

I settled myself on the couch with the latest copy of *Farm Weekly*, but I couldn't stay focused on the article about alpaca grooming, nor the one about the best way to grow your own tomatoes. My thoughts kept wandering after every sentence I read, zooming in on Justin. Why did I care about him being here? And why did his arrival feel like such a shock? High school was a long time ago.

I chucked the magazine aside and turned on Netflix, pulling up *In Dire Need*. If Justin was the star Suzie claimed he was, I had to check it out.

Of course I'd heard people talk about *In Dire Need* before, but I had always assumed it was some stupid show that only aired on one of those obscure channels. Townspeople here often got excited about things that were completely mundane.

So yeah, I had never realized how popular the series was. I hardly had time to watch TV or go to the movies. I mostly played old nineties series in the background while catching up on housework. If I didn't, the loneliness had a way of creeping up on me and taking me by surprise. Kind of like Justin Miller.

I pushed play on the first episode, half expecting it to suck. But when Netflix asked me if I was still watching *In Dire Need*, it dawned on me that hours had passed since I'd so much as moved.

I rolled my neck from side to side, trying to ease the cramps that had appeared from sitting in the same position for hours.

Nothing about his performance made sense to me. In the series, Justin came across as the sweetest, sexiest specimen alive. Seeing his character on screen even made my heart pound a little faster. Yet in real life, he was a jerk.

I turned off the TV and stared into the dark. Why had I even watched an entire season of that show?

As I slid under the covers, I couldn't get Justin out of my head. Or at least, his character Gabriel Finch. He was a great actor, I'd give him that. But there was no way in hell I'd ever admit that to him.

Get your copy of
LOVE TO PROVE YOU WRONG
and keep on reading!

Note to my Readers

Thank you so much for reading this book! It means the world to me and I hope you enjoyed it. If you have a minute, I'd be really grateful if you left a review for Snowflakes and Sparks. Reviews help authors so much!

Want to receive a free book, updates and a chance to be a part of my ARC team? Subscribe to my newsletter at http://www.sophieleighrobbins.com. I send out newsletters once a week and always keep them concise as I know time is valuable!

Feel free to follow me on social media to get a look behind the scenes, see what I'm up to, check out giveaways or get book recommendations. If you post about my books, make sure to tag me and/or use the hashtag #sophieleighrobbinsbooks.

Acknowledgements

No book is written in a vacuum. So many people helped me make this book into what it is, and I'd like to thank all of them.

First of all, a big thank you to Kirsty McManus. I really appreciate and love your friendship, help and feedback. I'm lucky to have you!

Thank you to Rachel Olsen for helping me make this story better and richer with a thorough development edit.

Thank you to my amazing editor Serena Clarke. I'd be lost without you! I'm so happy we get to work on my books together.

To Brooke, thanks so much for all your valuable feedback, the songs you select for me and the support you offer. I deeply appreciate all of it.

To Vikkie, thank you for your support and your amazing reviews. You're the best.

To Evie, thanks for being a great beta reader and book cheerleader.

To my family and friends for cheering me on, celebrating my milestones with me and reading my books and support me in any other way: a big thank you.

To my grandmother, for helping me reach my dreams and supporting me, even though you don't know the first thing about digital publishing. You rock!

To all the bloggers, ARC readers and authors who spread the news about my books: a big thank you.

To all of my readers: thank you so much for reading my stories. You guys make my dreams come true.

And as always, an enormous thank you to my amazing husband. Your unfaltering support means the world to me. You stand by me every single step of the way, and the stuff you create for me rocks. Plus, you keep me alive by cooking me amazing meals. I love you.

ALSO BY SOPHIE-LEIGH ROBBINS

The Best of You

Snowflakes and Sparks (Old Pine Cove #1)

Love to Prove You Wrong (Old Pine Cove #2)

In For a Treat (Old Pine Cove #3)

231

Printed in Great Britain
by Amazon

25796233R00136